ILLINKY

ILLINKY

High School Basketball
in
Illinois, Indiana, and Kentucky

EDITED BY
NELSON CAMPBELL

The Stephen Greene Press/
Pelham Books

THE STEPHEN GREENE PRESS/PELHAM BOOKS

Published by the Penguin Group
Viking Penguin, a division of Penguin Books USA Inc., 375 Hudson Street,
New York, New York 10014, U.S.A.
Penguin Books Ltd., 27 Wrights Lane, London W8 5TZ, England
Penguin Books Australia Ltd, Ringwood, Victoria, Australia
Penguin Books Canada Ltd, 2801 John Street, Markham, Ontario, Canada
L3R 1B4
Penguin Books (N.Z.) Ltd, 182–190 Wairau Road, Auckland 10, New
Zealand

Penguin Books Ltd, Registered Offices: Harmondsworth, Middlesex, England

First published in 1990 by The Stephen Greene Press/Pelham Books
Distributed by Viking Penguin, a division of Penguin Books USA Inc.

10 9 8 7 6 5 4 3 2 1

Library of Congress Cataloging-in-Publication Data
Illinky: high school basketball in Illinois, Indiana and Kentucky/
edited by Nelson Campbell.
   p.   cm.
   A collection of stories, some original, some reprinted from local
newspapers.
   ISBN 0-8289-0754-4
   1. Basketball—Illinois—History. 2. Basketball—Indiana—
—History. 3. Basketball—Kentucky—History. 4. School sports—
—Illinois—History. 5. School sports—Indiana—History. 6. School
sports—Kentucky—History. I. Campbell, Nelson.
GV885.72.I3I44   1990
796.323'63—dc20   90-35465
                                                           CIP
Printed in the United States of America
Set in Palatino by CopyRight, Bedford, Mass.
Designed by Deborah Schneider
Produced by Unicorn Production Services, Inc.

CONTENTS

PART III: KENTUCKY 125

ACKNOWLEDGMENTS

Special thanks go to Scott Johnson of Mahomet, Illinois, a high school sports historian by avocation, who helped immeasurably in unearthing material and reviewing the manuscript.

Thanks are also due fellow journalists Pat Harmon of Wyoming, Ohio; Kenn Hess of Portland, Oregon; Brad Holiday of St. Louis, Missouri; John McGill of Lexington, Kentucky; and Don Peasley of Woodstock, Illinois, who provided both material and encouragement.

Still others made contributions similarly appreciated: Mildred Blake, Ted Caiazza, Roy Conrad, Ron DeBrock, the late Charles Durham, Mike Embry, Bob Frisk, Larry Hawkins, Bob Pruter, Richard Rabbitt, Toney Roskie, Don Schnake, Herb Schwomeyer, Dolph Stanley, Ruth Stuessy, and Charley Vaughn.

PREFACE

Basketball, the most totally American sport, is one of our most vibrant common denominators. It reaches deep into regional cultures everywhere.

Its appeals and flairs are essentially the same whether in city ghetto, farm town, or suburb. Basketball is the most democratic U.S. team game because it requires the least personal expenditure, opens its doors the widest, and excites people in all walks of life: young and old, boys and girls, rich and poor, urban and rural, black and white.

While basketball's volume of literature pales before baseball's, the court sport has a vast untapped reservoir of compelling legend and lore. These reach their fullest flower in the high schools, perhaps the last bastion of athletic purity. They reflect the folkways of North, South, East, and West, yet fall into a common American crucible.

With the entire nation as its milieu, the 1988 anthology *Grass Roots & Schoolyards* assembled some of the best high school basketball literature of the past 50 years. *Illinky: High School Basketball in Illinois, Indiana and Kentucky* probes deeply into the rich lore of Illinois, Indiana, and Kentucky, three contiguous states where the sport most nearly approaches religion. This is the Midwest/Near South region that produced George Mikan, Isiah Thomas, Doug Collins, Terry Cummings, and Andy Phillip from Illinois; Oscar Robertson, Larry Bird, John Wooden, Rick Mount, and George McGinnis from Indiana; and Joe Fulks, Frank Ramsey, Wes Unseld, Dave Cowens, and Darrell Griffith from Kentucky.

This book seeks to share the best basketball stories from the "religion" states.

FOREWORD

This is a book that tells the story of basketball as it was played in the small towns and cities in Illinois, Indiana, and Kentucky. It doesn't generalize. Each town, each city has a story, and these stories go beyond the world of athletics. They are about schools, athletes, and the communities surrounding these athletes.

I grew up in the city and I heard of basketball in the small towns, but I never had it brought home to me so vividly as in this book. Some of these small towns produced championship teams with meager enrollments and poor facilities. Stars were born in the small towns as well as in the cities.

I enjoyed the book, and I am sure you, the reader, will, too. You will enjoy the happiness, the sadness, and the tragedies that go hand in hand with basketball. This is life, not fiction.

The death of Ben Wilson shocked the sporting world. The story is here: his life, his death, and the reaction of the community.

If you like basketball, or if you like sports, you will enjoy this book.

— Ray Meyer
Head Coach (retired)
DePaul University

PART I

ILLINOIS

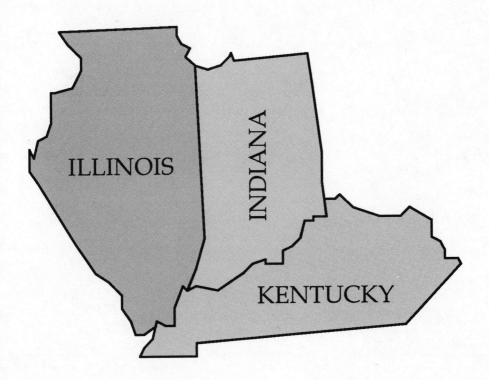

EVERY DAY IS SUNDAY

Basketball can be a unifying force in a community,
whether the atmosphere be triumph or tragedy. It has
worked both ways in Teutopolis, a town of 1,400 along
U.S. 40 in southeastern Illinois perhaps best known
for its colorful team nickname, Wooden Shoes. The
force was supremely evident in 1986 when both boys'
and girls' teams from Teutopolis High won state Class
A championships. It was perhaps even more evident
when a star player was killed in an auto accident and
3,000 people passed by the casket in the school gym.
The priest in this predominantly Catholic town once
said that because of basketball, every day is Sunday in
Teutopolis. "Wooden Shoes?" It stems from a local
shoemaker's gift to Coach J.H. Griffin in 1935. Mike
Eisenbath of the St. Louis Post-Dispatch *wrote this*
story after a journey to T-Town in 1987.

On a bright, unseasonably warm February day, this town of 1,400 in central Illinois seems to be taking a nap. At least, all seems quiet from the city limits.

Someone is drinking a Coke at the Dutch Treat restaurant and gazing out the window at Route 40. A couple of people are picking out a movie down the road at "Titletown Videos."

From the center of town, the steeple of St. Francis Catholic Church keeps a protective watch on the folk below. Majestic isn't the word for this church; comfortable is much better. It is estimated that more than 95 percent of the people in the community attend and identify most stages of their life with this church. The people of Teutopolis, for the most part, are Catholic, conservative, and clean-living.

But beneath the passive demeanor there burns a passion.

It involves basketball, which is part of life's fabric in Teutopolis. Basketball and the high school gym are as much a part of life here as the town mill and the church and the Knights of Columbus hall.

On this February day, fourth-grader Todd Starwalt and seventh-grader Brent Swingler are playing a heated game of one-on-one on Brent's

3

driveway. Todd is a little taller, but Brent has a nice shot and is rather feisty on defense. A block away, four boys are playing on another concrete court.

"I'd be very disappointed if I didn't make the basketball team when I get to high school," Todd said. Brent dribbled while Todd talked. "I don't miss many of their games. Only if I have to baby-sit, or if I get sick, or if my mom isn't home."

Last year Teutopolis High became the only school in Illinois sports history to win boys' and girls' state basketball titles in the same season. Emotions are running high as both teams try to defend their titles.

It's February Frenzy, and it will turn to March Madness. But basketball fanaticism is nothing new to T-Town at any time of year.

"If they have basketball in heaven, Teutopolis will be in charge," said Father Vitus Ducinski, the pastor of St. Francis. "There's no place like this in the world. Every day is Sunday. I love it."

Ducinski has been in Teutopolis for six years after stints in Ohio, Texas, and St. Louis. He may be an example of how well a diocesan personnel office can match a priest to a community; he already was a big Boston Celtics fan before he arrived in T-Town.

Teutopolis Wooden Shoes basketball is more personal than the National Basketball Association, however. The gym takes on the festive air of a wedding reception on Tuesdays and Fridays when the boys' team plays at home. Eighteen hundred people, packed to the rafters, yelling and screaming.

Three or four times a week during the winter—the girls' team draws pretty well, too—the whole town gets a night out. Teutopolisians have been doing it for years.

"It's this way all the time," said girls' coach Dennis Koester. "People live and die basketball in Teutopolis all year. I think they'd get a big following if you took two kindergarten teams and had them play.

"There have been an awful lot of moms and dads in this town that played at Teutopolis, and they've been very good. I'm sure when all my girls on this team grow up, they'll be in the stands. Six-month-old babies in the stands now will be there 30 years from now with their kids."

T-Town basketball teams almost always rewarded their supportive fans with good seasons. Last year was beyond their wildest dreams, however. The boys became only the 13th basketball team in Illinois history to go through the season undefeated. The girls won their championship in their fourth consecutive trip to the Elite Eight in Champaign.

This season was projected as a letdown. All five starters from the 1985–86 girls' team graduated. Four of the boys' starters and the first four off the bench from the '85–86 squad graduated, too. Most schools would call it rebuilding.

The Wooden Shoes call it reloading. The Lady Shoes are 23–1 after a victory in the sectional semifinals in Teutopolis on Wednesday night. The boys are 19–3 and ranked among the top 10 Class A teams in the state; their regional tournament will begin Monday. T-Town is cheering louder than ever for its Shoes.

"I watched Ted Smith at T-Town when I was little, and he was my idol," said Rich Hartke, a starter on the boys' team. "I don't really think of myself as an idol, though, but I do get a kick out of the kids in town. They all know you when you're on the team and wave at you whenever you go down the street."

Last October 12, two cars rolled up opposite sides of a hill on a narrow country road outside Teutopolis. It was dusk. The road was barely wide enough for two cars, even if both drivers could have seen each other approaching.

The cars collided at the top of the hill.

The 19-year-old driver of one car was killed. Three members of T-Town's basketball team, going home after a day of hunting, were in the other car. Tim Smith suffered a split kneecap and didn't return to the lineup until just after Christmas. Russ Nieburgge suffered an ankle injury and didn't get back into the lineup until mid-January.

Todd Kroeger, a 6-foot guard who started as a junior last year and figured to be the top player on this year's team, was killed.

"We have very few problems in this community; it's a family-oriented town, and I have yet to meet a kid who is a mean kid here," Koester said. "But we have a lot of tragedies. There are a lot of traffic deaths for a small town.

"Of course, it's always a tragedy when someone dies so young. But Todd Kroeger was a super young man. Something like that shocks a community, and it pulls them together."

In a community that cheers for its basketball players with the vigor of a family encouraging a toddler's first steps, Teutopolis was overwhelming in saying good-bye to Todd Kroeger.

There was no funeral home capable of accommodating all the people who wanted to pay their last respects. So Kroeger's casket was viewed in the high school gym. The scene of so many of the thrills of his lifetime and the focus of so much of his effort became the site of a testimony to the spirit of the community.

About 3,000 people silently walked into the building to kneel beside Kroeger's casket. They were lined up winding into the hall, out the door, and onto the sidewalk along Route 40. There was standing-room only for a rosary in the gym later. The church was filled for the funeral.

"We had coaches from teams we play bring their whole team to the gym for the wake," said Ken Crawford, the boys' coach at Teutopolis for six years. "Everyone came together in that gym, the whole town."

But the loss of Kroeger didn't seem to hinder the basketball team.

"Our feeling was this," Crawford said. "If Todd would have been here after something like that happened, he would have said, 'Let's pick up and play the game the way it's supposed to be played.' He wouldn't have gotten down. He would have tried that much harder."

"Success breeds success," said Ron Probst, who played on the '66 Teutopolis team and now hopes that his three grade-school-age children eventually will play for T-Town. "We've always had a rich program, and it has just gotten richer because we have come to expect excellence. As fans, we're all uptown coaches, we all think we're coaches. But it's like I heard one of our coaches say, we're quick to criticize but we're also quick to compliment."

In a small town, you immediately hear both.

"Everybody knows everybody here," Probst said. They ought to; they've been seeing one another at basketball games and church for years.

"But you know," added Probst, "they always say in a small town there's nothing else to do. I don't buy that. Basketball and church are the top priorities, but I don't think there's anything you have in St. Louis that we don't have here or can't go to quickly. We have the same problems of any community."

Problems don't have time to grow when the whole community is watching. Basketball helps serve as a rally station.

Lawrence Carie is the station master. He's the athletic director and was the boys' basketball coach for 23 years before handing the reins to Crawford. He also is the father of Doris Carie, who was named Illinois's Ms. Basketball last season in leading the T-Town girls to the state title.

"I decided that maybe I ought to take the time to watch my kids play basketball instead of missing it while I coached," Carie said. "I told the Lord one day that if my daughter won a national Elks hoop-shooting contest, I'd quit. She went out and became the first girl ever to make 25 out of 25 free throws in 1980 at the national contest in Indianapolis. So I quit."

Carie has statistics on how crazy T-Town is for basketball. He said there are 150 reserved chair seats that have been held as season tickets since 1971, and the only way to get them now is to inherit them.

Come April, though, life here will slow down drastically.

"After the season, we'll lower the rims around town to eight feet and play 'dunk ball,' and we'll pretend like we're pros until August," Rich Hartke said.

"When the season is over," said Dennis Koester, "everybody goes and finds himself a set of golf clubs. I get me a fishing pole and find a quiet spot by a lake. A lot of people will really support their kids in softball and baseball leagues. It really is a family-oriented town."

And if the Wooden Shoes make it back to Champaign, you can be sure Teutopolis will empty out that weekend.

Said Phil Hartke, a starter on the '65–66 team and Rich's father: "The biggest thrill for us was last year when Rich put on that gold state championship medallion around his neck. He pointed at us into the stand when he did it. He said he was there for us."

THE GOOD OLD DAYS

*The most delicious basketball recollections aren't
always related to important games played in big
arenas and covered by city newspapers. Many of them
simply reflect grass roots conditions and thus show
how deep the game runs in American culture. Those
from "the old days" may astonish youngsters who
have never known anything but relatively luxurious
facilities. They may also shatter the old-timers. What
could make one feel more ancient than outrageous tales
from bygone eras? However, past basketball generations,
particularly that of the Depression, produced many
inspiring scenarios that brought out the best in
our people. Here is a potpourri of recollections, from
sublime to ridiculous, gleaned from all sections
of Illinois.*

On the tail end of a fast break the shooter delivered what looked to be
an easy lay-up. But no. It fell off, and the home team grabbed the rebound.
The lad deserved a better fate. He was the victim of an occasionally successful hometown ploy. The backboard on that 68×42 floor was held in place
by iron pipes projecting from the wall and accessible to balcony fans.
Shaking the pipes at the key moment while directing an ear-splitting
scream at the perhaps unsuspecting shooter just a few feet away prevented
at least a few enemy field goals.

This was a 1948 scene in the town hall gym at Clayton, an Adams
County village of 800 population and a high school enrollment of 49. But
it might have occurred in any of the scores of tiny not-yet-consolidated
Illinois high schools. Most of them also functioned with makeshift athletic
plants, undermanned but often outstanding squads, and coaches who
wore many hats and had their private aces in the hole. Prep basketball
tales, not necessarily old, not necessarily outrageous, have long spiced
community life in the heartland.

Consolidated in 1951 with Golden and Camp Point into Camp Point
Central, Clayton said a gradual good-bye to its picturesque town hall arena.

It featured a stage at one end, end lines next to the walls, a cannery in the basement, and a one-spigot shower (visitors first, referees last, assuming they stuck around). During the first consolidation year, the team practiced in Camp Point's town hall gym, spread 10 home games among the three schools, fielded a first five comprising at least one player from each community, and logged 3,500 miles to and from practice sessions. A year later the Camp Point gym, seating 150, became the exclusive home floor.

Old-time Adams County fans swear there were soaped rims at Mendon Unity. There was a cement floor at Canton, Missouri, across the river that guaranteed sore legs for days if not weeks. And there was a radiator in a corner of the Plymouth gym up in Hancock County. If a player received a hip in that sector, he could expect a burn.

A decade earlier, in Henderson County 25 miles north, depression economics had taxed the make-do ingenuities of school officials even more. Terre Haute High had 36 students, four teachers including one athletic director-coach, and a less than half-size gym that was used as a study hall during the day. The floor could have fit crossways on a regulation layout. At practice time three dozen desks were pushed into the halls and classrooms. On game nights an elevated stage midway along one side, closed off with a folding door and used as a classroom during the day, was opened up for spectator chairs and an officials' table. The stands consisted of a single line of chairs around the gym. Any lurch out of bounds meant landing in somebody's lap.

The Terre Haute high school games were preliminaries of double-headers. The windup featured the town adult team. One official handled both games for a fee of five dollars. Travel to Tri-County League games at Oquawka, Stronghurst, La Harpe, Little York, Media, Gladstone, and Burnside meant piling in private cars driven by the principal and one or two teachers. The cars carried the players, two cheerleaders, balls, uniforms, towels, and, during the winter months, a scoop shovel. The only insurance was that of the car owners.

Retired coach Stan Walker recalls that he received $1,200 a year to teach four subjects and coach two sports. He remembers zone defenses plugging those crackerbox gyms, deafening noise in close games, high-arch shots occasionally hitting the ceilings, and out-of-bounds plays starting under the balconies at Biggsville. Lack of decelerating room meant that after a driving lay-up, the player would either crash against a wall or be forced to stop short at the edge of a stage. None of the old Tri-County gyms are in interschool use today, and some have been torn down.

While Coach Walker has fond recollections of a 25-victory season, the real bottom line is that his students turned out well. They came from complete families endowed with the rural work ethic. Parents attended all school events and were supportive of teacher efforts. Contacts were close, teachers were respected, and they had more authority than they do today. It was a different time.

Weird tales of basketball physical plants abound in Illinois. A loose plank in the Carterville floor caused particular havoc in the twenties. If an unsuspecting visitor stepped on one end just right, he could be swatted by the other end. Or a dribbled ball could go awry. Even some of the larger schools—for example, Marion, the 1921 state champion—had crackerbox gyms well after World War II. The Marion sidewalls were inches behind the court lines, and its low ceiling thoroughly cramped the stratospheric "kiss" shooters of conference foe Centralia. In the old days they played on stages, in barns, in town halls. There were running tracks and other overhangs serving as impediments to shooting, rickety floors, soft spots best known to the home team, and floors where authorities, believe it or not, also permitted roller skating.

The state's tiny gyms included a 74×34 layout at Hebron, a situation that drove Coach Russ Ahearn to schedule all except six of his games away from home during the 1951–52 championship season. Cregier High on Chicago's West Side has perhaps the best-known throwback to the crackerbox days. Only a little over 75×27, its dreaded court has been the scene of numerous home team victory totals of 125 points or more. Among the most memorable were three thrashings in the 1984–85 season—143–76 over Juarez, 142–96 over Lincoln Park, and 134–88 over Wells. In a previous gym, short and fat instead of long and narrow, Cregier had run up a 152–51 count on hapless Prosser. The game was punctuated by the winners' 75 field goals, 44 first-quarter points, and a hand clock allegedly let run too long.

Tied to afternoon games in ancient gyms before small crowds during the regular season, today's Chicago Public League teams look eagerly toward invitations to downstate holiday tournaments, shoot-outs, or single games. There they attract big crowds, achieve statewide recognition, and put more money in school coffers than they might realize all season at home. Dan Davis, former Crane coach and Northwestern player, once contrasted suburban and Public League basketball facilities as "the difference between Heaven and Hell."

As late as 1982, Milford High in Iroquois County installed an indoor-outdoor carpet as playing surface. The old cracked tile floor needed replacement, but school officials blanched when they received a $100,000 new-floor bid. The $14,000 price tag on brown carpeting was easier to stomach. The good news was that the local Bobcats won most of their games on the strange surface despite so-so overall records. The bad news was that the ball had a dead bounce. When a player took a fall, he'd better roll or suffer a rug burn.

Scoring trends? Consider the dark winter of 1930. Georgetown nipped Homer on an early free throw, 1–0. Magnolia nipped Hopkins of Granville, 1–0, on a late free throw. Rossville defeated Catlin, 5–0, in one overtime while Wenona edged Tonica, 6–4, in four. Canton had won the 1928 state tournament final over West Aurora, 18–9.

Fouls? It used to be 4-and-out. Now it's 5-and-out, and some think there should be no banishment at all. They advocate simply adding penalties for infractions beyond 5. In the 1952 DeKalb holiday tournament, unlimited fouls were allowed. Hines of Kirkland and Blair of Monroe Center each amassed 10.

Coaches? They've always been central figures in controversy or lingering yarns. In 1962 the Valmeyer coach, upset by Freeburg's running up the score, instructed his players to hand their opponents the ball. Valmeyer lost, 105–41. On the other hand, various Illinois coaches have played three or four men in deference to opposition reduced to similar circumstances due to foul-outs.

Officials? They try not to make news but can't always control the situation. On March 3, 1958, they called 50 fouls on Mount Carmel in a Chicago Catholic League game against St. Rita. With nine players fouled out, Mount Carmel finished the contest with three players and lost, 84–70. In 1952 a game between Hennepin and Lostant ended with only two on two. A 1906 contest between Phillips and Armour Academy in Chicago was called on account of noise! The referee awarded the affair, 10-all at the time, to Armour! In 1913 the Lane Tech (Chicago) janitor turned off the gym lights and locked the building during a game with Senn. The police had to be called to spring the crowd.

Fans? In 1939, as a show of support, a hundred Benton fans and the school band walked six miles to the West Frankfort regional. Their team defeated Johnston City, 23–21. Forty-five years later a state regular-season record 10,400 watched Peoria Manual play Pekin in the Peoria Civic Center.

Transportation? It could be gamy. In February 1965 the Beason bus, on the way home from a district tournament, was stranded 14 hours overnight by a blizzard. In 1929 the Rockbridge team, stymied by spring floods that made roads impassable, hopped a railroad handcar and pumped its way to a game at Greenfield six miles away.

Tournament organization? There weren't enough large gyms in the old days. At the same time, the postseason tournaments were moneymakers. The results were some unusual qualification rules. From 1936 through 1942, both district and regional runners-up advanced to the next level. Thus it was possible to lose twice and stay alive. Five teams survived this double loophole—Hampshire (1936), Indianola and Nebo (1939), and Melvin and Palestine (1942). County tournaments added to the rivalry duplications. Allerton and Sidell met seven times during the 1936–37 season. First-round IHSA tournament mismatches provided the impetus for introducing the regional tournament in 1936, then separating all schools into Classes AA and A in 1972. Scores such as Joliet's 136–5 massacre of Mokena, Olney's 107–13 conquest of Parkersburg, and Moline's 110–12 destruction of Coal Valley, all in 1935, helped speed the former thrust.

Altercations, disputes, and litigation? History records plenty of each. Even 1908, the year the first state tournament was played in the Oak Park

YMCA, produced a major flap. Rockford was invited to the Oak Park event but declined, in part because of hard feelings stemming from a brawl after a Rockford-Oak Park football game a few months earlier. Rockford thereupon met Washington in an unsanctioned "state championship" game and won.

But this was only part of a much larger brouhaha. Rockford and Peoria, the eventual official champion, seemed to have the best credentials in 1908, but they were at loggerheads, too. One of the Peoria stars, William Forrest, was a transfer from Rockford. Prior to 1908, "state championships" were determined on a challenge-the-claimant basis. Now challenged by Peoria, Rockford also declined this invitation, advising Peoria to first meet Washington, the school from which the Rabs had wrested the "title" during the 1906–07 season. Peorians were insulted by this. They felt their team was clearly superior to arch-rival Washington, a two-time loser to Wheaton. There would be no "play-off game" for the right to meet Rockford.

The site wasn't the only problem affecting Rockford's attitude toward the official tourney. There was also a date problem. Rockford had a home game with Washington on what was to be the first day of the state event. As the big event drew near, Peoria lost to crosstown rival, Spalding, and Rockford partisans chuckled. After Rockford left the floor in protest after its game with Mt. Carroll ended in a tie, Peoria papers called the protagonists "cowardly." Meanwhile Washington accepted an invitation to the state tourney. Double-crossed, Rockford held Washington to its contract. Washington thereupon withdrew from the state tourney and on March 28 lost, 57–21, at Rockford in Illinois's last unsanctioned "state championship" game. After Peoria had won the official title, Rockford resurrected a late-season Peoria proposition that the teams meet on a neutral court in Ottawa "to settle things." With the official trophy in hand, Peoria was no longer interested.

Other brouhahas flash to mind.

When 13 Argo players revolted in December 1969, presenting a list of demands, the school board suspended the boys for a year and the athletic department forfeited the season. The board favored leniency but bowed to the wishes of the teachers, who said they'd leave their jobs in that event.

Who can forget the St. Michael's fiasco? The Chicago school, ranked Number 1 in Class A in 1977, lost by one point to Walther Lutheran in regional play but sued in district court on the basis of an apparent scorer's error. The judge ordered the second half of the game replayed, and St. Michael's lost again by one point.

In 1981 a district court allowed the wearing of Orthodox Jewish yarmulkes (skullcaps) by members of the Ida Crown and Yeshiva high school teams in Chicago and Skokie, respectively. There had been an IHSA rule prohibiting the wearing of "any head gear or head decorations" in games.

Back in Adams County they remember the limbo between segregation and integration. As late as 1952, an interstate tournament across the river in Hannibal, Missouri, barred blacks if a Missouri team was involved but left their use optional if Illinois teams met each other. Things changed the next year. Lots of things have changed.

A STAR IS DEAD

Life in the black ghettos has always been harsh and cheap. Passage to and from school is often fraught with danger. When you grow up in the streets, the watchword is survival. It took the emergence of black athletes by the multitudes to reveal the reality of ghetto conditions to much of the outside world. In 1984 Ben Wilson, a marvelously gifted junior, led Simeon High School from Chicago's South Side to the state Class AA championship. At the start of the 1984–85 season he was Number 1 on virtually everybody's national college prospect list. He had a sure ticket out of the ghetto. Then on November 20, 1984, he was murdered by another teenager within sight of the school. Had he lived, he would have been a Simeon teammate of Nick Anderson and Ervin Small, a potential that boggles the mind, and perhaps with them on the University of Illinois's Final Four team in 1989. Memorable words were written about the life and death of Ben. The best appeared in the Philadelphia Daily News, *740 miles away. They were written by former Chicago sports columnist John Schulian, who knew the South Side well. His work, which follows, was adjudged one of the best sports stories of 1984 by* The Sporting News.

The news was like death itself. Someone ran up and said Ben Wilson had been shot, and the next thing Bob Hambric knew, he was racing out the door and down the street, not quite believing that any of this was happening.

Hambric was Ben's coach, the surrogate father who had overseen the growth of a skinny, clumsy freshman into the nation's foremost high school basketball player, and every step he took jumbled his emotions a little more. "I was in a fog," he says, "but then I saw the school policeman hustling out there, too, and I knew there was trouble. He's used to panic."

So Hambric moved even faster, increasing the distance between himself and the elementary school students he had been introducing to the wonders of Simeon Vocational, the students who were supposed to hear Ben Wilson speak next.

And Ben Wilson lay on the gritty sidewalk half a block north of Simeon, felled by two bullets from a .22-caliber Ruger revolver and numbed by shock.

He was propped against the wire fence next to the A&A Store, where he had come on his lunch hour with two girls to wander amid the video games and school jackets. Simeon's football coach was giving Ben first aid by the time Hambric reached his side, and inside the A&A a student was describing how it had happened, Ben bumping a stranger and saying, "Excuse me," and the stranger telling the kid with him to shoot Ben. It was the Tuesday before Thanksgiving and a dream had been shattered.

Now the school policeman was trying to hold back the crowd that was spilling out into Vincennes Avenue. A crowd—how ironic. Ben Wilson always drew a crowd. He was 17 years old, and what he could do with a basketball meant that he was forever surrounded by teammates, admirers, and recruiters. They filled his ears with the sound of adoration, but in these tortured minutes, he couldn't hear a thing.

Maybe it was just as well. The air was flooded with the wailing of sirens and grief. "The kids were crying," says John Everett, the pro football official who flexes his muscles as an assistant principal at Simeon. "I broke down, too." But Bob Hambric held his ground, refusing to let the tears inside him fall, waiting for his world to stop spinning out of control.

He looked for a pool of blood, saw none, and took heart. The wound that was visible in Ben's side seemed almost harmless, just a puncture in his windbreaker. "I was thinking the kids he played with would have to learn to get along without him for a while," Hambric says. They could start that very afternoon, in fact, when a photographer from *USA Today* was scheduled to take their picture as the Number 1 high school team in the country. There were plenty of pictures of Ben that could be sent along later.

That was the only consolation Hambric could find as he watched Ben being placed in an ambulance. The attendants worked with the practiced haste of men steeled by the random cruelty on Chicago's South Side, and yet they still overlooked one thing, Ben's blue-and-white stocking cap.

Hambric picked it off the sidewalk, flicked the dirt off it, and put it in his pocket. He figured Ben would need the cap when he came home from the hospital.

They say this city has never seen a funeral to equal it. More people turned out when Mayor Richard J. Daley died, and the same was true of the passing of Cardinal Cody, the archbishop of Chicago. But Ben Wilson was a kid.

He wasn't a politician who built an empire by trading jobs for votes, and he wasn't a religious leader who weathered controversy by showering his flock with blessings. Ben Wilson was a black basketball player with a golden future. He was someone for his people to rally around in a city where not being white can still get you chased from your home, chased into the bitter night.

So they came to say good-bye to Ben Wilson, both the family and friends who had known him as "Benji" and the strangers who had merely seen his name light up the sports page. There may have been as many as 8,000 of them at his wake in Simeon's 600-seat gym. "They were three deep for something like six hours," John Everett says. "At one time the line stretched for two blocks. It was unbelievable." And the funeral was even more so—perhaps 10,000 mourners crowding inside and outside the headquarters of Operation PUSH, the civil rights organization, before Ben Wilson was laid to rest.

The swell of emotion was as startling and heart-tugging as his mother's courage. Five hours after her son died at dawn on November 21, Mary Wilson stood before a student assembly at Simeon and said, "I know hatred can never return good. I'm just sad. I don't feel hate for anyone."

Whatever chance there was for hatred must have been eliminated by sorrow when Mary Wilson listened to the doctors tell her how badly her son was hurt. She is a nurse, which means she has listened to those droning, unemotional voices before, but now the wounds she was hearing about were in her son. One of them was his groin—no problem. But the other had struck his aorta. "When they told Mrs. Wilson that," Bob Hambric says, "I'm sure she knew right away how serious it was."

It was serious and it was wrong, the way every senseless shooting is. But there was something that made the killing of Ben Wilson worse yet, because it violated one of the unwritten rules of inner-city life: Athletes are off limits to violence. They are the ones who have a ticket to better places, and they are not to be deterred by either gangs or free-lancing thugs.

Simple geography should have reinforced that premise at Simeon, for the school is surrounded by a steel mill, a 7-Up bottling plant, and an assortment of warehouses. There is no neighborhood for a gang to call its turf, and when houses finally do come into view, they are clean and solid, a proud statement that the rules of decency are meant to be obeyed.

But every time Coach Hambric's friend, Mike Washington, thinks of the two 16-year-olds charged with Ben Wilson's murder, he knows how little all of that meant. "Those guys," says Washington, "broke the rules."

And they ended a story that shimmered with happiness.

In the beginning, Ben Wilson was a project. He came to Simeon on the coattails of a better player, a player who was stronger and faster but couldn't live up to the academic and athletic demands that Bob Hambric put on him. He flunked out, but Ben Wilson stayed.

He wasn't just skinny then; he was short, too. Somehow, though, Hambric saw beyond those 5 feet, 11 inches. "I'd always wanted a big guard," the coach says, "and I thought Ben could be it." Nobody else understood why when they saw Ben flopping around as the last man on the freshman-sophomore team.

"He didn't even start a game, and Coach Hambric was always talking about how great the kid was going to be," John Everett says. "I just shook my head and said, 'Good luck, Coach.' "

But luck didn't make Ben Wilson the player that Indiana, DePaul, Illinois, Georgetown, Iowa, and Michigan were fighting over. Oh, maybe you could argue otherwise after learning that he grew to 6-3 by his sophomore season, and 6-7 as a junior, and 6-8 going on 6-9 this year. "You could almost see him growing when he was walking down the halls," Hambric says. The measuring tape didn't shoot 150 jump shots a day for Ben, though, nor did it jump rope for hours, run mile after mile, or soak up everything his coach told him.

"Ben was special," Hambric says, "and I felt I was special because I was chosen to guide and train him. There was a natural attraction between us. We did things together, went to shows, played basketball Sunday mornings with the old guys I usually run with. Ben did all his studying in my office at school, and if he wasn't studying, we'd talk about things. I'll probably never have another player like that."

The reasons are as obvious as the Illinois state championship that Simeon won last March, and as obscure as the day Ben Wilson discovered what he could be. Hambric had the varsity practicing at one end of the gym, and he wanted to make a point to a senior guard who was loafing. "So I looked down to the other end of the gym and hollered, 'Ben, come here,' " Hambric says. "Ben came down, got a couple baskets, did what I wanted him to do. I thought it would make the senior angry, but he just laid down right there. I asked Ben, 'You want to stay here?' and he said, 'Yeah, yeah.' He didn't leave until he had no choice."

In between, he laid the foundation for Simeon's current 34-game winning streak and convinced the prestigious Athletes for a Better Education to name him this season's premier player. It was an honor that escaped Isiah Thomas and Mark Aguirre and Terry Cummings and all the other big names Chicago's high schools have produced in the last decade. Maybe Ben Wilson earned it because he covered more of the court than any of them did.

Whenever fouls hog-tied Simeon's center, Ben would move into the middle and throw his 185 pounds around as recklessly as he could. If there was trouble against the press, he would bring the ball upcourt, using his height to see over the defense. Sometimes, however, he made you forget about his size.

"He was always able to maintain the ability of a small person," Hambric says. "He could drive to the basket and fold his body up. There wasn't a crack he couldn't get through if he needed to."

And yet the way to remember him is standing tall. Think of the game he played against Corliss High School last season when Hambric had benched two starters for missing practice and Simeon trailed in the first half by as many as 10 points. "Ben just rose up over everybody else," Hambric says. In the process, the deficit shrank to 3 points, and then to 1 as Ben dunked an offensive rebound. A heartbeat later, he was blocking a shot at the other end of the floor and taking the ball back to where he could unleash the last second jumper that won the game.

That was Ben Wilson as he seemed destined to be forever—unstoppable.

He was buried in his traveling uniform. His mother will hang the new home uniform he never wore in his closet. His coach gets the ski cap and the game film from last season that he didn't think he'd have the courage to watch.

"I thought at one point I would just erase them," Bob Hambric says. "I guess I'll have to buy a new case of tape instead."

That way, he can always have Ben Wilson.

It is something everybody in Chicago is trying to do now. They will retire Ben's number 25 at Simeon in the spring, and when the school builds a new gym, it will be named after him. Money is coming in from across the country for a memorial fund to aid Ben's family and the two-month-old child he fathered out of wedlock. Scarcely a day passes when a newspaper story doesn't point out that Ben was just 1 of 90 young people Chicago has lost to gunfire this year, and in City Hall politicians of every persuasion are grinding their axes on the tragedy. So much tumult, so much shouting, but some things never change.

In front of Simeon Vocational, its doors locked by a city teachers' strike, a kid dribbles a basketball. How old can he be, 11, 12? He feints and whirls, even flicks the ball between his legs as he works his way past the school and toward the spot where Ben Wilson was stopped by two bullets.

Surely the kid knew who Ben was. Maybe he is even imagining himself as Ben in full blossom. But you will never get anyone to believe that he can hear Ben's coach saying, "Tomorrow isn't promised to you," or that he understands he is traveling on a street of broken dreams. And that is as it should be.

Reprinted from John Schulian, "Only the Good Die Young," *Philadelphia Daily News*, December 7, 1984, p. 144. © With permission of the Philadelphia Daily News.

HOTBED

High school basketball is serious business in small midwestern towns. It's a balm during the long, sometimes harsh winters, and a five-player team sport gives the small school at least a fighting chance among the mighty. Basketball also becomes a means of establishing community identity. Benton, a southern Illinois coal-mining community of 6,800, is a classic hotbed. Once better known for football, the local Rangers have been a consistent basketball force for more than two decades. Their four boys' Elite Eight appearances in the past 10 years were divided equally between Classes AA and A, a quirk made possible by a borderline enrollment averaging about 740. The school's best-known hardwood products are Olympian and NBA star Doug Collins, Rich Yunkus of Georgia Tech, and Wilbur Henry of Illinois. Frederick Klein captures the Benton flavor in this 1971 Wall Street Journal *feature.*

Dave Lockin, a pleasant, well-mannered boy who stands 6-feet, 7-inches tall, is the leading scorer on Benton High School's basketball team, averaging 15 points a game. The ball goes through the hoop about two-thirds of the time he shoots, and he's a good rebounder to boot. Still, people here speculate somewhat sadly on how skillful ol' Dave, a senior, might have been if he'd been brought up properly in Benton.

"You see, Dave comes from a little place in Kentucky and never got to play any real competitive ball until he moved in here as a freshman," explains Richard Herrin, the Benton High coach. "Our boys start doing that earlier—usually in about fourth grade."

Such dedication is a big reason why Rich Herrin's Benton Rangers won 24 of their 25 regular-season games and now are given a good chance to win the state high school basketball championship, whose initial phase gets under way tonight. Since the 37-year-old Mr. Herrin came here to coach in 1960, this southern Illinois coal-mining community of 6,800 has enjoyed all the distinction that comes with schoolboy basketball success in an area that is a "hotbed" of interest in the sport (the residents themselves use that term). The team is "a real source of local pride," beams Howard Payne, president of the Bank of Benton. "When you've got a winner everybody knows where you are from."

In its preoccupation with basketball, little Benton is like towns all around rural Illinois, Indiana, and the rest of the Midwest used to be 15 or 20 years ago. For such small communities, which lack symphonies, museums, art galleries, and sometimes even a movie house, high school basketball was one of the few diversions during the long winter evenings, a rare source of color and excitement and one of the few ways to make a civic reputation. In Illinois, towns such as Pinckneyville, Paris, Herrin, Hebron, and Mt. Vernon—not the sort of places that usually attract attention—established indelible and vivid identities by producing teams that went "all the way" to capture the state title.

By and large, small-town people don't get as worked up about prep basketball as they used to. They now have television sets and superhighways, so the local high school team has to compete with other entertainments. "People are getting finicky," says a sports editor in a central Illinois town of 10,000, where 3,500 fans used to pack the local gym for every home game but where such turnouts now are rare. "The only way to get people out now is to have a big winner," he notes.

At the same time, "big winners" are getting more scarce among small-town teams as the tide of prep basketball dominance has shifted with the population to the cities. In Indiana, long considered the nation's capital of the small-town game, the last three state champs have come from the steel-making cities just southeast of Chicago or from Indianapolis, the state capital, and East Chicago Washington High is heavily favored to win this year. In Illinois, Chicago-area teams have won four of the last five titles, as many as in the previous 24 years.

It's still possible for a little town to have a state champ, of course; "it's just that we have to work a lot harder," says Coach Herrin. If Benton High, enrollment 714, doesn't make it this year, it certainly won't be for lack of work by players or townspeople. The town has organized basketball teams down to the sixth grade, where the squads include the best players from lower grades. Intercity competition begins at grade seven. Two weeks ago a full house of 1,300 showed up at Benton's WPA-built gym to watch the town's eighth graders play a state quarterfinal game.

For the Ranger varsity, there is nothing but the best. The squad has all manner of workout equipment down to a device for practicing tip-ins that pops the ball out of the basket once it goes in. When the Rangers take to the road, they wear matching gold blazers and carry travel bags of the maroon-and-white school colors. Since midseason, the team has been the proud possessor of a videotape machine bought by the school and a group of local businessmen. Before, the team had to make do with a movie camera to film games for instructional purposes.

Townspeople find various ways to pitch in. Mrs. Marge Battle, who runs Battle's Grill on the town square, gives free malteds to players who make all their free throws in a game. Charley Smith, who says he runs the biggest retail coal yard in the U.S., has "Go Rangers" signs on his trucks. The team is mentioned favorably from the pulpits of the town's churches.

Some in Benton think the team gets too much attention. Barnie P. Genesio, the school's principal, is a former basketball coach himself who took a team from little Shawneetown to the state tournament in 1955, and he declares he's "just as big a duck in the puddle as anyone else" when it comes to rooting for the Rangers. Yet he displays a letter announcing that Paula J. Budzak, a Benton High senior, is a National Merit scholarship finalist, and he says "the newspapers come to us about our basketball team, but we have to go to them to get them to use this sort of thing."

"In this town, the tail (basketball) wags the dog," says the father of one Benton High pupil, who says he doesn't want to be identified "because that sort of view isn't too popular here." He adds: "Money that ought to be going to education goes to basketball. Kids who don't play the game might as well not exist. It's got all out of proportion."

Coach Herrin doesn't agree. "People who say let's downgrade athletics ought to realize that the whole world is competitive. If people can't compete in sports, they'll compete to see who has the best band or something else," he says. Besides, "teaching good sportsmanship and character is a lot easier if you're winning than if you're getting beat all the time."

Rich Herrin was raised in a series of small southern Illinois towns where his father served as a Methodist minister; Benton is the largest city he has lived in. He is earnest in manner and is a regular churchgoer. He doesn't smoke or drink. He talks with the part-Southern, part-Midwest rural accent native to his home region.

Ever since he was a boy, his main interest has been sports. In this, he says, he takes after his older brother, Ron, who now coaches high school basketball at Olney, Illinois, about 70 miles north of Benton. He says that both he and his brother took after their father, now retired in Olney. "Dad would have been a big league baseball player if he'd been willing to play on Sundays," says Rich. "He could throw a good curve ball when he was 50."

Rich was neither fast nor big—he didn't reach his full height of six feet until he was a senior in high school—but he practiced a lot and eventually became a good athlete. He went to tiny McKendree College in Lebanon, Illinois, near St. Louis, because he could continue to play varsity sports there. He still holds the school's single-game basketball scoring record of 47 points.

Coaching, he says, "is all I ever really wanted to do. When I started in college, I thought maybe I'd be a dentist, because Ron was going into coaching and I thought one coach in a family was enough. But after a while I figured, heck, why should he have all the fun?"

Rich's first coaching job was in Okawville, a southern Illinois town of less than 1,000 residents whose high school had an enrollment of about 200. In four years, his basketball teams there won 95 games and lost 17.

When he came to Benton in 1960, the school had a reputation of being good in football but mediocre in basketball. Such situations usually are created by the personality of a coach, and Rich turned it around. To date, his Benton teams have won 221 games while losing just 90. They have won the South Seven Conference title four times: the school had never won it before he came. Three of his teams—in 1961, 1966, and 1967—advanced at least to the final 16 in the state tourney.

Rich says that there are "no secrets" to the game of basketball; "all the coaches have about the same amount of technical knowledge." The trick, he says, "is to motivate the boys to do the work that's required to win. Teen-age boys do whatever is popular in their town. I had to make basketball the thing to do."

Rich says he was "lucky and fortunate" that his first team at Benton was a good one; it started the season poorly but perked up enough at state tournament time to get all the way to the quarterfinals before losing in overtime. After that, he says, "I had a whole string of real fine boys who worked their tails off to be good players. They set the style for the little boys who were coming up." He adds: "I guess I've had more than my share of tall boys, too. You can't coach a boy to grow."

Coach Herrin also has had a more direct hand in Benton's basketball ascent. His teams have a reputation for being poised and well drilled. They play a thrusting style of offense, his guards leading fast breaks when they can and otherwise seeking to get the ball to the big men underneath the basket. Their defense usually is man-to-man and always is tenacious.

The coach has instituted several measures to set his players apart from (and, hopefully, above) their rivals. One is the traveling bags and blazers; "they make the boys look sharp and feel proud," he says. Another is a team rule that all players wear their hair crew cut. "A couple years ago, a bunch of the players came to me and said they thought it ought to be a rule that everybody have a crew cut," explains Rich, who wears a crew cut himself. "I got nothing against longer hair—I even grew some side-burns this summer—but I figured if the boys voted on it, crew cuts were okay. Now we got a bit of a tradition going. The day after Thanksgiving, all the players go get their hair cut and the local paper takes pictures." Anyway, he goes on, "short hair probably is good for their basketball. A boy that's on the court messin' with his hair isn't thinking about the game."

From time to time, rivals have complained that Rich has helped his cause by recruiting players from smaller nearby communities. This is against Illinois high school rules, and the coach denies that he does it. Still, he says, "if a boy's daddy comes to me in my home and says he thinks his son has good potential and could benefit from the kind of tough competition we have, I won't run him off." Benton High has had "two, three kids who've moved in and helped us" over the past few seasons, he notes.

Besides coaching basketball at Benton High, Rich Herrin, a father of three boys, teaches three classes a day in driver education and is the school's athletic director, track coach, and assistant football coach. For all of these tasks he is paid $15,200 a year. He earns an additional $1,500 a year by running the school's summer driver education program and picks up several hundred dollars a year more by appearing at summer basketball camps and clinics.

Sought-after prep coaches have been known to receive various lucrative fringe benefits from their grateful communities. But while Benton is grateful and Rich Herrin is sought after (he's turned down numerous offers to coach at other high schools and even a few college bids), he says he doesn't get anything much on the side. "But people here have been very nice to me," he quickly adds. "When I built my new house this summer, some folks came out and helped. They've helped out in other ways, too, over the years. I guess that's just because they're friendly."

Rich Herrin's current team is unlike some of his previous ones in that it has no single "star" to carry the scoring load. Instead, it has a balanced offense with six players averaging between 8 and 15 points a game. It has good rebounding and the usual tough Herrin defense.

High school basketball at Benton is staged with all the flourish of the big time. About 600 of the 1,100 seats in the school's gym are sold on a reserved, full-season basis. The rest go on sale the evening of the game and are snapped up well before the preliminary game between sophomore teams starts at 6:30 P.M.

The Benton varsity takes the floor to the tune of "Sweet Georgia Brown," the theme song of the Harlem Globetrotters, which is belted out by the school band. (There's a certain irony in the use of the same song as the Globetrotters; both the Benton High team and the town are all white. Negroes haven't been especially welcome in the southern Illinois coalfields since they were brought in as strikebreakers in the bloody union organizing days of several decades ago.) The team performs a couple of snappy running and ball-handling routines before beginning its pregame shooting practice. Before the game, each starter is introduced to the crowd individually with appropriate fanfare.

The seriousness with which the coach takes a game is obvious. His pregame instructions are punctuated by shouts of "Let's go," to which his team responds with staccato clapping. Rich tries to keep himself under control during a game, but the tension breaks through often. His favorite outlet is banging his heel violently into the floor; the area in front of where he sits is deeply marked from such blows.

On a recent Saturday morning, facing a game with arch-rival Mt. Vernon in the evening, Rich calls the boys to the gym at 10:30 to do a little light shooting and to view the videotape of the previous night's game in which they beat Carbondale, 68–51.

That night, in the Mt. Vernon gym, where they haven't won since 1968, the Rangers lead by as much as 27 points and wind up winning 77–60.

On the way home in the bus, Rich Herrin muses about his team's state tourney hopes. "We've got the balance, and the boys are smart so I don't think they'll get rattled when the pressure gets up, but I wish they had more of a killer instinct," he says. "They can't seem to go out and play real aggressive ball for all 32 minutes. They usually let up somewhere, and that could hurt us."

At the city limits, the team bus is met by a town police car with its siren on and its dome light twirling. Thus escorted, the bus is driven twice around the empty town square in a lonely victory procession.

"Just wait until we win a big one in the state, though," says Rich Herrin. "There'll be 1,000 to 1,500 people standing out there in that square. Boy, it'll really be something."

"HE MADE US
STATE-CONSCIOUS"

*On rare occasions a reporter's personal story is as
compelling as that of any of the individuals he writes
about. This story is about such a man. Taylor Bell of
the* Chicago Sun-Times *called him the original
basketball junkie, but he was more than that. He was
the consummate newsman who found new insights
along the byways of a state extending farther north
than Boston, farther south than Richmond, and
farther west than St. Louis. He saw in Illinois's
"Sweet 16" and its unique network of Christmas
holiday tournaments a vast untapped field for
coverage. He wasn't a native of Illinois, he doesn't
live in Illinois, and he hasn't worked in Illinois since
the Truman administration, but he is an integral part
of Illinois sports growth, high school basketball in
particular. Here is a small segment of his story.*

What Illinois sportswriter did more than any one person to develop state-wide high school coverage and create the statewide consciousness we know today? If you're over 50, you'll have the answer on your first try. Even if you're a generation younger, you may know it because your parents told you.

Pat Harmon.

It's Harmon hands down, even though he left Illinois 43 years ago for new opportunities in Iowa, then Ohio. It's Harmon, even though his primary milieus as sports editor of the *Cincinnati Post* were major league sports rather than their high school and university counterparts in Illinois. People remember.

Pat went where sportswriters had never gone before, and from teenage years on, he came up with ideas that delighted the increasing statewide readership of his *Champaign News-Gazette*. It was he who as a high school boy picked Illinois's first recognized all-state basketball team. It was he who first made the rounds of the holiday tourneys. It was he who researched newspapers from 1908 to 1931 in order to produce needed records for the state classic. It was he who coined the term "kiss shot," first seen at Pontiac, for the long, two-hand, high-arch deliveries of Arthur Trout's Centralia players.

An only child, Pat attended 18 schools—in Arkansas, Kansas, Missouri, Iowa, and Illinois—before entering La Harpe (Illinois) High. His parents were trapeze artists. His father died four months before Pat was born, and his mother died when he was 12. He had no relatives and was fortunate to be taken in by a family of kindly strangers who lived down the street in La Harpe.

It was at La Harpe High that Pat began his journalistic career. He had a secondhand typewriter that his mother had bought for one dollar. He contributed stories about La Harpe's basketball team to the local weekly, *The Quill*. He remembers those players for their appropriate nicknames: Tub Myers, Rabbit Fowler, Sock Long, Shady Landis, and Hunger Burkhart. (The man has a steel-trap memory, the kind that can quickly recall the first five of just about any team from his 60-year purview, the spot where a player was standing when he made a key shot, or the specifics of a long-ago conversation with a coach.)

Moving to Freeport High, Pat met Adolph Rupp just before he left for Kentucky and national fame. He wrote high school sports for the local *Journal-Standard* and went on scouting trips with the coaching staff. In 1932, at age 15, he won a free ticket to the state tournament in a *Bloomington Pantagraph* contest; he picked the most winners out of Illinois's 64 district tourneys. He hitchhiked to Champaign with eight dollars but no place to sleep. Fortunately he saw Sam Lifschultz in a sporting goods store. He had met Sam, a referee who had coached the state's first outstanding big man, 6-foot 8-inch Bob Gruenig, on one of the scouting trips. Sam arranged free lodging at his brother's fraternity house.

Back in Freeport, Pat began to study the sports sections of the Illinois papers that came in each day. He noted that no one had ever picked a true all-state basketball team, only all-tournament teams limited to players from schools appearing in the "Elite 8." The time had come. For his inaugural honor five in 1933, Pat chose Lou Boudreau of Thornton and Lester Tammen of Kankakee, forwards; Bump Jones of Freeport, center; and Lowell Spurgeon of Centralia and Wilbur Henry of Benton, guards. Three (Boudreau, Jones, and Henry) became Big 10 regulars while a fourth (Spurgeon) opted for football, also becoming a Big 10 regular.

Enrolling at the University of Illinois in the fall of 1934, Pat faced a new set of problems. He had an $80 tuition scholarship arranged by the sports editor of the *Journal-Standard*, but that was all. He got a part-time job under sports editor Eddie Jacquin at the *News-Gazette* for $4 a week, waited tables at Prehn's Restaurant, and did a little work for Mike Tobin, the university's sports information director. His room rent was $6 a month.

He performed marvelously in the college courses he liked and more or less ignored those he didn't. Journalism was his love. He got better and better at it, and soon his employers realized what a jewel they had. Certainly his price was right.

It was Jacquin's idea to do occasional features on prep teams likely to qualify for the state tournament, a Champaign (University of Illinois) fixture since 1919. Pat was the man for the job, and the Christmas holiday tournament circuit would be the inaugural vehicle. What better way to observe lots of contender teams in one swoop?

Armed with $10 in advance money, Pat set out for De Kalb and Pontiac, the most venerable of Illinois's holiday classics, each with a 16-team field. After that would come major games at Pekin and Quincy. Pat hitchhiked to the sites, slept on a cot in the De Kalb gym, ate meals with the teams at Pontiac, stayed at the home of Coach Frenchy Haussler in Pekin, and stuck with Boudreau and the Thornton team, the visitors at Quincy. Sometimes officials would take him to dinner. Sometimes coaches would line up rides for him with salesmen.

Back in Champaign, Pat returned $1.25 of his $10.00 advance, thus dramatizing one of the biggest freeloads in journalistic history. He had mountains of notes for features on teams adjudged to be state contenders. The Associated Press in Chicago had him do a series on all the good ones. In the process he picked Springfield and Thornton to be the state finalists. They were.

All this was in a deep depression year when conditions were so bad at the *News-Gazette* that regular staff members had taken three consecutive 10 percent cuts in salary. It was also a period unconducive to motorcades and gala community celebrations in the wake of state tournament championships. After rival central Illinois city Decatur produced the 1936 winner, Jacquin thought it would be innovative to do a community reaction story. Because there was no concerted response anywhere in town, Pat had to go into the players' homes to get his story. The same situation prevailed in 1937 when Joliet won. The big change came in 1940 when Granite City took the title with a team of predominantly eastern European extraction. Amid dramatic circumstances in that first year of the war in Europe, the players were escorted to Lincoln Place, their community center, and roundly feted. This time Pat's assignment was easier.

As the depression waned, things got better at the paper and hitchhiking to assignments became just a memory. Pat pushed statewide coverage even harder, and by the time he succeeded Jacquin as sports editor, he was well known from the cities and industrial towns of the north to the farms in the central section and the coal- and oil fields of the south. He saw the steadily increasing number of prep holiday tournaments (more than 600 Illinois schools participated in 1989) as performing an educational service by bringing together youngsters of different cultures and environments.

In the fall of 1943, Pat asked Coach Dolph Stanley of Taylorville how well his basketball team might do in the upcoming season. "We won't lose a game," Stanley replied. They didn't, finishing at 45–0 for the first unbeaten season in state history. Pat tried to arrange a game in the Chicago Stadium between Taylorville and Mount Carmel, champion of the Chicago Catholic League. Both Stanley and Mount Carmel coach John Tracy were agreeable, but since the Chicago school was not yet a member of the IHSA, the latter would not permit the game.

When Harmon was inducted into the Illinois Basketball Coaches' Hall of Fame in 1974, the committee solicited his views. He thereupon submitted a list of 26 perceived mistakes, including both people left out and people left in. Among those he thought should be in were coach-official Lifschultz and Lewis Omer, who as director of the Oak Park YMCA organized the first Illinois state tournament in 1908.

While Pat was an only child, he wound up superintending a family of 11. For years the Harmons' Christmas card pictured the youngsters lined up football style, 7 in front and 4 in back. Each youngster's jersey bore a number indicating his or her age. The "coaches," Pat and Anne, his wife since 1940 and college sweetheart, lined up on the sides.

Harmon retired from the *Cincinnati Post* in July 1985, but men of such energy seldom retire at an age as young as 69. Maybe they never do. Pat is now historian/curator of the College Football Hall of Fame in Kings Island, Ohio. How could they have found a better guy for a job like that?

A SPOONFUL
OF SUGAR

Next to the arts, athletics has perhaps American society's best record in providing universal opportunity. Better than business. Better than labor. Better than government. But the record isn't so wonderful. The state tournament in Illinois, the land of Lincoln, wasn't completely integrated until 1946, 38 years after inception. Even then, acceptance was slow. Generally speaking, the mainstream colleges recruited blacks only after they felt they couldn't win without them. For a while at least, their administrations could afford an ivory tower approach to minority problems. The high schools never could, and they deserve special credit. Their officials dealt with the basest of entrenched community emotions, and historians will probably say they did pretty well. This story resurrects a few pertinent Illinois scenarios along the way.

It was just after V-J day, and three veterans back from the hot spots were sharing overseas stories and making predictions for the Brave New World.

"There won't be any more wars," declared Number 1. "Maybe a few local skirmishes but no big ones. The United Nations will keep everybody in line."

With all due respect for some noble efforts and several peacekeeping missions in place at this moment, that prediction hasn't panned out too well.

"Technology will soar," said Number 2. "There'll be machines that catalog mountains of information. Just press a button and we'll save weeks of research."

That was a good one.

"Negroes will move high in all sports except those costing a lot of money," said Number 3. "They'll do particularly well in basketball."

"No way," snorted Number 4, good ol' Joe. "They'll never stand the pressure."

Number 3's forecast was bull's-eye, but, by the same token, Number 4 represented a widespread sentiment. Despite the great success of straight professional teams such as the New York Rens and the heroics of a few black members of predominantly white high school teams, the paying white crowds preferred blacks in the role of Globetrotter-type clowns and really did suspect the ability of blacks generally to withstand the hurly-burly of major high school and college play. Moreover the movers and shakers preferred the objects of their personal cheering to be white, whether by law, custom, or competitive selection. Otherwise enlightened universities that occasionally recruited black football players drew the line in basketball. They worried about visibility: gridders were heavily garbed and performed farther away. Besides, it was usually easy enough to find 12 good white basketballers.

Blacks played their role and waited for the winds to change. The first big influence was World War II. The second was *Brown vs. Topeka Board of Education* (1954). The road to integration was rocky, and some of the early episodes, whether perceived as heartwarming, maddening, or humorous, may astonish anyone under 40. In Illinois it took one of the most monumental high school upsets of all time—Douglass of Mounds over West Frankfort in 1946—to focus attention on a racial situation involving 7 of its 102 counties.

World War II had ended just a few months before the Illinois High School Association made its decision to admit previously barred downstate all-black institutions to postseason tournament play. If Negroes could fight and die for the U.S.A., then Negro schools should be eligible to participate in a mainstream educational activity, association officials reasoned. Prior to 1946, all-black schools in East St. Louis and Lovejoy (St. Clair County); Venice, Madison, and Edwardsville (Madison County); Mounds and Mound City (Pulaski County); Cairo (Alexander County); Brookport (Massac County); Carbondale (Jackson County); and Colp (Williamson County) had held their own district tournaments, with two survivors meeting in Champaign for their championship as part of the regular IHSA tourney program. All-black schools in Chicago as well as integrated schools in Champaign, Danville, Decatur, Peoria, Quincy, Galesburg, Moline, Freeport, Mt. Vernon, Centralia, et al., all longtime members of the IHSA, were not affected by the new dictum.

Feeling the necessity of a go-slow pioneer year because of "racial feelings" in the seven involved counties, the IHSA sent the two all-black district champions to "safe" regionals. They assigned the Carbondale winner, Douglass of Mounds, to Benton, 70 miles from the school, where fate decreed that its semifinal opponent would be West Frankfort (26-2), one of the top three teams all season in state rankings and owner of the only victory over eventual state titlist Champaign. They sent Madison Dunbar, winner of its local district, to Highland, 30 miles away, rather than to the nearest regional, Belleville. Therein lay the rubs.

Since few in the know expected either Douglass or Dunbar to seriously contend, it all seemed academic. The larger focus was at Benton where the well-drilled West Frankfort Redbirds, led by future Northwestern star Cotton Hughes, was the title hope of all southern Illinois. Douglass (23–4), winner of the state Negro tournament a year previous, eliminated Zeigler in the first round and opened a few eyes. Still few were worried; West Frankfort had all the ingredients of an outstanding high school team and was tournament tough.

The Douglass-West Frankfort game was downright epic. The Redbirds played their regular patterned game, shot well, got more shots *and* rebounds and led at the half, 23–19. But Douglass, shooting phenomenally from distance, won the game, 55–51. Protests, rumors, and barbs flew across the state. West Frankfort fans screamed at the presence of a team four regionals from its home. The IHSA defended its assignments by stating that (a) Douglass and Dunbar deserved to be in the tournament but that (b) it would not have been "practical" to send them to Cairo or Belleville. It was The Great Compromise. It didn't look good at the time, but who is to say it wasn't the best decision in the long run?

The upset provided a field day for speculators and wags. Who *were* these Douglass people? Were they a super team ready to stand "Sweet 16" fans on their heads? Was this a manifestation of the occasionally predicted "African athletic revolution?" Disguising their voices, jokesters called University of Illinois athletic director Doug Mills, announcing that they had the greatest team of all time, would be bringing thousands of fans to Champaign, and needed outrageous numbers of hotel accommodations.

What happened to Douglass after the West Frankfort miracle? Alas, not much. It was king for only a day. It lost the regional title game, 58–37, to Johnston City, which in turn bowed in the sectional. Meanwhile the IHSA ship was righted, and by the following year all its schools became subject to the same assignment considerations.

It was a welcome twist of fate that brought Charley Vaughn to little Tamms High School, just 18 miles north of Cairo and the Ohio River. This was 1954, the year of *Brown vs. Topeka*. He would become the state's all-time leading high school career scorer and watch his 3,358 points survive one onslaught after another for 32 years to date. A teenage basketball player won't sense that he is inching integration ahead in a once completely segregated community only a few miles from where the Illinois Central's Jim Crow cars once started, but Vaughn probably was. It has been said that a winning team, which Tamms had during the Vaughn era, can do wonders for brotherhood. A spoonful of sugar can make the medicine go down.

Tamms is a poor town, and there were many negatives for a young black. In 1958, his glory year, he still couldn't eat in Tamms restaurants. There were occasional epithets among crowds on the road. Once a little girl cried in fear. She had never seen a black person before. But he looks at the bright side. He remembers breaking the state record at home on the wings of 44 points, seniors crying at graduation, and the opportunities afforded him by basketball. He played at Southern Illinois University where he broke the school's career scoring mark, then labored eight and a half years in the pros, setting an ABA three-point field goal record with the Pittsburgh Pipers. He would love today's 19-foot, 9-inch college 3-point distance.

Vaughn, known as "Chico" to media and fans, became a folk hero when he returned to college at age 47 to complete degree work abandoned long ago. He was tired of hearing that he could have a given job if only he had a degree. If there were ever a quintessential advocate of athletes paying attention to education, it is Vaughn. He has some good memories of high school, particularly the enlightened ways of his principal, Stephen W. Clark. When school integration issues seared the atmospheres of numerous U.S. cities a few years later, Clark wrote a letter to a Chicago newspaper, suggesting that if a poor border school (then called Alexander County Central) could make integration work, larger and more resource-blessed city schools could also. Excerpts of the letter follow:

Dear Sir,

In view of all this hubbub concerning segregation and states' rights, I deem it a professional duty to present these facts in favor of integration.

In our high school of 200 students we have 60 Negroes. They have added tremendously to the overall school program. In addition, they have afforded the opportunity of putting into practice the fundamental doctrines of our democracy and of making our Constitution a living document workable on all occasions. The way the two races work and play together is a tribute to the teachings of our Christian faith.

Alexander County Central High School was integrated five years ago because of financial necessity. At that time there were many doubts as to the success of the venture. Now we are all convinced that it has worked and can be made to work in any community.

The community of Tamms is no different from any other border state community. We have just as much hate, jealousy and fear. We have been able to overcome these weaknesses by much patience and a moderate amount of democracy and Christianity applied through the medium of education. I recommend the same for other communities where integration is necessary. The multitude of evils that are attributed to integration approach the realm of fancy and actually should be no cause for alarm.

Sincerely,

Stephen W. Clark
Principal, Alexander County
 Central High School
Tamms, Illinois

The Douglass and Tamms scenarios may seem Stone Age reminiscences now, but they represented burning issues of their times and progress, however small, along the road to the democratic ideal. With school consolidations have come sounder academic institutions, more solvent entities, and stronger athletic teams perhaps at the mild expense of solidarity. Of the members of the old southern Illinois Negro leagues, only Lovejoy and much storied East St. Louis Lincoln remain. Douglass of Mounds has given way to Meridian, so named because the third principal meridian passes through the district. Alexander County Central is now Egyptian, so named for the "Little Egypt" region in which it is located.

In April 1989, just after Rumeal Robinson sank both his free throws with three seconds remaining to give Michigan a one-point victory over Seton Hall in the NCAA final watched by millions, good ol' Joe was spotted on a city street by one of the original quartet. It was the first time they'd seen each other in 25 years.

"Hey, Joe, how d'ya think those guys are standing the pressure?" the pal shouted across traffic.

Startled, Joe looked up at the sky, then smiled and shouted back, "My God, are we really *that* old?"

THE SCHOOL THAT
HAD EVERYTHING

*When veteran "Sweet 16" watchers gather 'round the
hot stove and rate the great teams of the past, there
are votes for Thornridge (1972), Quincy (1981), Mt.
Vernon (1950), Taylorville (1944), Chicago Marshall
(1958), Collinsville (1961), Paris (1947), and Lockport
(1978), all of which won, and Centralia (1941) and
Chicago DuSable (1954), which didn't. Somehow
unbeaten champion La Grange doesn't slip into the
conversation as often as it should. Perhaps this is
because it's a giant suburban school with so many
honors to its name. Perhaps it's because fate sandwiched
La Grange's heroics between two much-storied teams,
all-time darling Hebron (1952) and DuSable (1954),
the "greatest, blackest, saddest team from the meanest
street in Chicago." This story shines a well-earned
spotlight on La Grange of '53, a team that was
pressed only once—in what became known as "The
Battle of the Decade."*

The 1953 Illinois state final came earlier than usual. It wasn't part of the
"Sweet 16" at all. It was a sectional semifinal game, played in the grand old
Joliet gym on Herkimer Street. It attracted 5,200 fans, who crammed into
every nook and cranny of the 1923 structure. The date was March 12, and
the combatants were two undefeated teams that had alternated between
Number 1 and Number 2 in state rankings all season. One was La Grange
(Lyons Township), champion of the West Suburban League. The other was
Kankakee, champion of the South Suburban. Neither had been pressed,
and each had averaged a huge victory margin over its opponents.

Coached by Greg Sloan, whose interview remarks all season had fallen
just short of outright title prediction, the La Grange Lions (23–0) had outscored 14 conference foes by an average of 35 points a game, averaged
78 overall, and hit the 90 mark on five occasions. Their conquests included

33

a 70–46 rout of Moline just days after the Quad City team had won decisively over Davenport, Number 1 in Iowa, and previously unbeaten neighbor Oak Park, Number 5 in Illinois. Another Lion victim was perennial contender Morton of Cicero—by a whopping 82–39 in the regional final. Only New Trier, a 63–54 victim, capitulated by less than 10 points. Armed with great depth and one of the most versatile all-sport squads in national history, the Lions were led by muscular 6-7 junior all-stater Ted Caiazza, who had averaged 23 points despite the team balance and would three years hence play at the University of Illinois. It was said of La Grange's devastating defense that the boys started pressing you as soon as you got out of your cars.

Coached by Earl Jones, the Kankakee Kays (26–0) had averaged 77 points per game while limiting their opponents to 47, a record almost exactly that of La Grange. They featured 6-6 senior all-stater Harv Schmidt, who was averaging just under 28 points and would also later play, then coach, at the U of I. A Kankakee victory over La Grange, with the state championship clearly in sight, would have put frosting on the community's centennial celebration, but this was not to be.

Once the season had slipped into January, hardly a day went by that writers in heavily populated northeastern Illinois didn't speculate on the outcome of La Grange vs. Kankakee. The confrontation seemed sure to come because it would be only a first-round sectional game, and how could such juggernauts lose in regionals?

La Grange's supporting cast featured outstanding stars from four sports. Forward Joe McRae would go from high school to one of the Harlem Globetrotter teams. His brother, forward Leon, was an all-state back in football. Guard Nate Smith was a baseball catcher who would star in Triple A and play five major league games with the Baltimore Orioles. Reserve forward Harold Caffey was state 440 champion, would repeat two months later, and star in his specialty at Indiana University. Reserve forward Richard Caffey, Harold's cousin, was a hurdler who would set a state record in the 180-yard lows. Guard Chuck Sedgwick would play regularly at Bradley University, and the sixth man, guard Joe Lawlor, would captain the DePauw University team.

It was a feverish time for Coach Sloan, a fellow who actually liked football better and served as line coach in the fall. He had been flirting with the brass ring for several years. In 1948 his all-stater Jim Hoffman was hobbled after falling on the ice just before the regional, and the team, an early favorite, had to settle for fourth place at Champaign. In 1951 an unbeaten but fading Lion five was upset by Hinsdale, a nine-game loser, in the regional semifinals. Sloan's 1952 five, another good one, lost to Oak Park in the regional final. Each regional loss was by one point.

While Kankakee was back on top in the state rankings by sectional week, the majority of coaches and fans who had seen both teams play picked La Grange. Even the most lukewarm fans had an opinion. The volume of newspaper discussion was tremendous. To have a ticket to The Big One was like having temporary possession of the Hope diamond.

The game was all it was cracked up to be. The Lions drove on the Kays and won it from the free throw line, converting 37 of 53. Sedgwick contributed 16 of 19. Sloan's men also had a decisive edge in rebounds, 42–29. Schmidt outscored Caiazza in a memorable duel, 37–31, and brought down the house with some baseball-throw field goals. But while Schmidt hit from everywhere, the heralded Kay forwards Phil Werbiski and Dick Rapp were held in check, managing only three baskets between them.

The final score was La Grange 83, Kankakee 74.

The outcome was always in doubt, but La Grange led at every quarter and actually picked up steam in the final eight minutes. No one who saw the game or felt its hoopla beforehand will dispute the label "Battle of the Decade" that writers later accorded it. This was one year when the "Sweet 16" was anticlimactic.

Emotionally drained by the Kankakee struggle, the Lions were a little flat the next night against host Joliet, a team they had thrashed earlier, 90–44. They won by 11 and advanced to Champaign as heavy favorite.

Moved by stories using such phrases as "perfect team," "incredible depth," and "murderous press," many observers were mildly disappointed at La Grange's "Sweet 16" showing in old Huff Gym. Some of them had expected a combination of Kentucky and the Minneapolis Lakers. Still the Lions were never headed. By an 85–68 margin they defeated Chicago DuSable, the team that would make history the following year. They routed Decatur St. Teresa by 27 points, with Caiazza setting an all-time tournament single-game scoring record, 38. They eliminated Pinckneyville, the Number 2 pretourney choice, by 13, then Peoria Central in the final by 12. Never in serious trouble, the Lions had won four championship games by an average of 17 points and become the state's third undefeated titlist in 46 years. On the philosophical side, partisans asked, "What more did the team have to do?" On the practical side, they conceded that their team had reached its pinnacle on the night of The Big One in Joliet—when it needed to.

Sedgwick likes to recall the circumstances of Caiazza's record-setting basket against St. Teresa. He knew Ted needed two points to break Max Hooper's mark, but Ted didn't. Sedgwick had two free throws. He made one, then called a huddle. He missed, and Ted had three tips. The third went in, and he received an ovation from both spectator sections.

Although blacks constituted only 3 percent of La Grange's student body, they constituted 60 percent of the starting 5 as well as the first 10. It was a joyous period for residents of the community's East Side. Old-timers, who still regaled willing listeners with the heroics of Laurie Williams, an all-around black athlete at La Grange in the twenties, pondered the long odds that so many outstanding black athletes would appear on the scene at the talent-rich school at the same time. Drawing from several diverse communities, La Grange High School ranked high in virtually everything. For athletics there was the mixture of La Grange with its East Side, La Grange Park, Western Springs, the Congress Park section of Brookfield, some unincorporated area, and blue-collar industrial McCook that had produced football greats Lou Saban and George Paskvan. By the end of the 1952–53 year the 1,950-student school was state champion in basketball, track, and debate. The track and debate titles were repeats. If there had been state football play-offs at that time, La Grange would have been one of three or four 6A or 5A favorites.

One might not expect the large, well-off suburban schools to labor under any athletic disadvantages, but La Grange's conference had a few. In 1953 member basketball teams were permitted only three practice days a week. Too, the frosh-soph coach was often just as tenured as his varsity counterpart, thus ran a relatively private preserve and might effectively resist the commandeering of his players to varsity level.

La Grange made the "Sweet 16" again in 1968 but didn't return to Champaign until 1970, a glory year that rivaled '53. Led by Owen Brown and Marcus Washington, this team also fashioned an unbeaten season, winning the final by 19 points and establishing La Grange as the only Illinois high school ever to post two perfect basketball seasons. The '70 team has vocal advocates who press for its inclusion on any list of great state champions. They like to recall the huge letters on the side of a building along La Grange's main drag after the '70 triumph: "Bring on UCLA!" But the '53 team somehow stood out from the crowd. It had a special chemistry, a pioneering sparkle, a quiet killer quality, a stunning versatility, and a defense that seemed to shove opponents right out of the gym.

If you get in a bull session about Illinois's greatest high school basketball teams, give La Grange of '53 a fair hearing, will you?

LA GRANGE (83)

	FG	FT	R	F	TP
J. McRae, f	6–14	4– 8	10	5	16
L. McRae, f	4–15	3– 5	12	5	11
H. Caffey, f	1– 1	0– 0	0	0	2
R. Caffey, f	0– 1	0– 0	0	3	0
Caiazza, c	10–21	11–15	14	4	31
Sedgwick, g	1– 8	16–19	4	2	18
Smith, g	1– 1	0– 0	0	5	2
Lawlor, g	0– 7	2– 4	2	2	2
Johnston, g	0– 0	1– 2	0	0	1
	23–68	37–53	42	26	83

KANKAKEE (74)

	FG	FT	R	F	TP
Werbiski, f	2– 4	4–8	3	4	8
Rapp, f	1– 3	2–3	3	5	4
St. John, f	3– 8	1–1	8	4	7
Polk, f-c	1– 2	1–1	1	4	3
Ferrias, f	0– 0	0–0	0	0	0
Schmidt, c	16–31	5–7	9	5	37
Bertrand, g	2– 8	6–9	3	5	10
Weller, g	0– 2	1–1	0	2	1
Johnson, g	0– 0	3–3	1	5	3
Christopher, g	0– 0	1–2	1	0	1
	25–58	24–35	29	34	74

LA GRANGE	28	17	17	21	—	83
KANKAKEE	21	21	17	15	—	74

THE SCHOOL THAT HAD EVERYTHING

"BEAUTY GONE AWRY"

Dolph Stanley is an American Original. A coach's coach. A basketball legend in a basketball-rich state. His more than 1,200 high school and college victories over a 52-year period bridge the generations—from deliberate offenses with a larger ball in crackerbox gyms to lightning tempos in giant arenas. His trail winds from a Depression crossroads in southern Illinois to Madison Square Garden, from corn country and coalfields to city neighborhoods and the halls of a "little Harvard." Few coaches have so served across the complete institutional spectrum: college as well as public, private, and parochial high schools.

Stanley was coaching Johnny Orr when Ray Meyer was coaching George Mikan. He ran the "four corners" before Dean Smith was born. He perfected the slip-and-roll before it had its name. He used a zone press as early as 1934 and a full-court press as early as 1943 when few thought they would work. He made the "tipping zone" a devastating weapon. He pioneered the pregame handshake and player numbers both front and back. He took five schools to Illinois's "Sweet 16"— Equality (population 830), Mt. Pulaski, Taylorville, Rockford Auburn, and Rockford Boylan. His 1944 Taylorville team, led by Orr and Olympian-to-be Ron Bontemps, compiled a 45–0 record, won the state final by 23 points, and became a springboard for the storied Stanley creed that stresses conditioning, fundamentals, self-confidence, and gentlemanly behavior.

On the college level Stanley was the central figure in what legions of Chicago fans over 50 consider the most electric local game of all time. His 1951 Beloit Buccaneers, averaging under 6–1, put on their customary "Globetrotter" warm-up, then gave an interception clinic to rout a good DePaul team, 94–60, and earn an invitation to the NIT.

A head coach until age 82, Stanley came out of retirement twice, ending his career at Keith Country Day School, Rockford, in 1987. Among his storehouse of memories are his own final full-court game—at age 65—and the night of February 24, 1924, when he scored all of Marion High School's points in a 12–8 overtime triumph at Johnston City.

While Stanley says he "never invented anything," that he "only stole from the masters," legions of Illinois and neighboring state coaches freely admit they "stole" from him. The people at Rockford Auburn named their gym after him. Beloit College has named a room in its new sports complex in his honor. A plan to name the Taylorville gym after him is in the works. Listen to Mr. Stanley's proposals for the future of basketball as set forth in this 1988 article. Whether or not you agree with him, they'll stimulate your thinking. Even our dearest institutions need occasional examination.

"Why do you want to be a coach?" George Huff asked me when I was a student at the University of Illinois. "You'll never be rich."

He was right if you're thinking in terms of money. But if you're thinking in terms of personal rewards—the kind that come from forging good teams out of the rawest material or steering impressionable young men and women toward meaningful lives—he was dead wrong.

I've coached most sports, including football for three years, but most of my life has been a love affair with basketball. It's a beautiful, fluid game that reveals a mountain of athletic skills. But it's a game that's becoming ugly. As players get taller and taller, there's more and more mayhem under the basket and officiating is becoming tougher. The three-point field goal, which I advocated when it wasn't the most popular cause, has helped some. It opens up the "mass" zone defenses, encourages coaches to play more man-for-man, and creates greater excitement. But problems remain. This is a good time to look down the road and consider some basic changes.

Because basketball has undergone many radical alterations and the pressures on its players are great, I tend to divide my thoughts for the future into two big questions: "What's good for the game we love?" and "What's good for the young men and women we lead?"

First, the game. When you argue my proposals, remember I'm advocating changes in some of the very rules I helped write. Some major proposals follow:

1. **Do away with the five-foul disqualification.** Instead leave the offending player in the game and assess a strong penalty for additional fouls, such as automatic possession or one free throw plus possession.

2. **Eliminate the charging foul except when it is intentional.** Coaches and most fans know what "intentional" means. Let's don't continue to reward acting. For every "fullback plunge" toward the basket under current rules there are 10 Academy Award performances in which the carefully trained defensive player thrusts himself into the driver's path, often falling for good measure, and thus draws the "charge." Let the defenders be real defenders, not master deceivers.

3. **Consider eliminating all time rules after the ball is in play.** Even the 10-second rule is meaningless today. The 3-second rule, formulated more than 40 years ago to put extra motion into the game, is often flagrantly violated and has to be a drag for the much harassed officials.

4. **Allow no hand-checking.** Basketball is a noncontact sport.

5. **Add a third official for all college and pro.** Under present rules there is simply too much going on, particularly around the basket, for two officials to keep under complete control.

6. **Force the coach to remain on the bench.**

7. **Enforce strict eligibility rules.** The primary purpose of college and high school is education. We do a long-term disservice to young men and women if we allow them to slide academically.

    And now for a futuristic proposal that is sure to stimulate heated debate:

8. **Eliminate the backboard, suspend the hoop from the ceiling, consider extending the floor at each end to facilitate scoring from all directions, and widen the playing surface.** This combination would place a new premium on shooting and passing skills, open up the game, eliminate much of the heavy-traffic shoving now typical of basket-area play, and severely reduce the importance of the dunk, a flourish that I feel detracts from the game's beauty.

    For economic and legislative reasons these proposals are not likely to materialize soon. They may never materialize. But basketball deserves constant rules scrutiny if it is to reach and maintain its fullest flower. It deserves long-term thinkers as well as short-term.

Forget the record book and ask yourself what is really sacrosanct and what is really good for the game. College basketball got along without the three-point field goal for 94 years, but in 1986 it was approved by the NCAA. It was an idea whose time had come. A center jump after each goal was mandatory for 45 years, but nobody today would dream of reinstituting such a rule. Free throwing has undergone numerous transformations: one-player-take-all, the out-of-bounds option, and 3-to-make-2, all since discarded. The hoop is 10 feet high simply because the railings for Dr. Naismith's peach baskets were 10 feet above the floor in an age when a six-footer was a big man.

In my utopian vision I'd like to see the dunk outlawed completely, the zone defense outlawed at the college level, and traveling rules enforced more rigidly. While there are those who regard the dunk as a thrilling art form, I can't bring myself to appreciate a two-foot rifle shot from above the basket by a seven-foot player who frequently gets away with shifting both feet before launch. Someday a boy will be killed by hanging on the rim. As to defenses, the man-to-man makes for a more attractive game and gives the really skillful player more chance to shine. As to traveling, frontliners must be watched as closely as the guards. With all due respect to the great pressures on officials, dunkers and other inside men are violating "steps" all too often.

So much for the game. Let's turn to those who lead. What's best for them?

The coach is a major force in the lives of young athletes during a critical period, the years from ages 13 to 21 when they approach Fool's Hill, when they desperately need leadership and indeed are groping for it, whether they admit it or not. It's therefore imperative that school boards seek strong leaders for their coaching positions, men and women whose philosophies extend far beyond the won-and-lost columns. Pay more attention to the task of selecting coaches!

In providing leadership for their students, those who hire are accepting a solemn challenge or should be. They should consider the process a long-term investment in the country's future rather than simply a means of hammering out a state tournament team. Our young men and women are the future. We all want to win—coaches, principals, superintendents, board members, and taxpayers alike—but winning without commensurate leadership for life is shallow and misses the coaching ideal. Championships and cheers fade away, sooner than fans realize, but the real rewards remain.

We don't know how many young lives we've helped organize and point toward successful careers, but we know we've pointed quite a few. We don't know how many boys we've saved from prison, but we know we've saved some. I've had my own share of rewards and look forward to many more. For example, I look to the day when society realizes that coaches, like artists and musicians, improve with age. Meanwhile I've watched my players become positive forces in their communities and livelihoods. I've watched my game become truly international. I've watched my profession reach higher and higher status. This makes it all worthwhile.

TAXPAYERS TO
THE RESCUE

*The smallest school ever to reach an Illinois basketball
final was not Hebron (1952) or Cobden (1964) or
Flanagan (1983) or Venice (1987) or Hume Shiloh
(1989). It was Ohio, the 1986 Class A boys' runner-
up. The Ohio story transcends school athletics. It is
the story of a community's struggle to preserve its
identity and a way of life.*

When the Ohio Bulldogs, out of a 69-student Bureau County high school,
astonished Illinoisans by winning runner-up honors in the 1986 Class A
state tournament, fans from Rockford to Cairo wrinkled their foreheads
and asked a question: With all the consolidation talk over four decades,
were there still schools *that* small?

When they heard that the 116-year-old community of 550 subsidizes
the property taxes of new residents, that all its school referendums pass,
that the school lockers don't have locks, and that volunteers plow house-
holders' driveway snow for free, they pictured Ohio as a cross between
Camelot and "The Little House on the Prairie."

There were, and are, numerous tiny Illinois high schools, notably in
the more affluent Corn Belt and particularly in Bureau County. While the
public high schools of Indiana and Kentucky with fewer than 100 students
can be counted on the fingers of one hand, Illinois had 51 as late as 1989.
Bureau County, with only three-tenths of 1 percent of the state's population, contained 4 in addition to Ohio—Neponset (42), Wyanet (72),
Manlius (76), and DePue (83). Tiskilwa (113), LaMoille (123), Buda Western
(139), and Walnut (145) weren't much larger.

The big picture is that as families leave the farms and populations in
the farm towns dwindle, school consolidation is a continuing necessity.
As the merger pace has increased, so has the number of under-100 schools.
But they stem the tide in Bureau County. The residents are willing to foot
the higher tax bills occasioned by the loss of enrollment-based state aid.
The cost per student at Ohio Community High School was $6,379 at latest
report.

To a point, Ohio is a rural bedroom community, a comfortable, close-knit village where one can live while working in small industry at county seat Princeton, Spring Valley, Walnut, or Manlius. Since its population was aging, the subsidy program was conceived as a way to reverse declining school enrollments and avoid consolidation. The program allots $5,000 to buyers of new homes in Ohio and $3,000 to purchasers of existing homes. These allowances generally cover five to three years of taxes. The subsidy stems from the nonprofit Ohio Growth Foundation, originally spearheaded by two local businessmen and funded by 25 of their neighbors.

Keeping a high school in traditional form can be a tremendous solidarity factor in a small town. Once it is closed or consolidated with other schools several miles away, the community loses much of its identity and, in the minds of some, its reason to exist. The Ohio people sought to allay all that. Despite the high cost and a student body with only 12 freshmen, they're holding the fort.

Ohio holds a lofty position in area basketball that goes back five decades. The Bulldogs won seven district championships under the one-classification system and have earned four regional Class A titles under the two-class system. They reached the "Sweet 16" in back-to-back years, 1985 and 1986, posting an overall 55–6 record during that span. They are a frequent champion of the 13-school Indian Valley Conference, whose ranks include Wyoming and Bradford of Stark County, Annawan of Henry County, and Tampico of Whiteside County in addition to the 9 Bureau County schools.

Ever since the 1986 heroics in Champaign, the name "Ohio" has struck a magic chord. In 1987 the Bulldogs played the preliminary to a Quad Cities Thunder pro game in Moline's 6,000-seat Wharton Field House. They whipped Tampico, 82–62, and the *Bureau County Republican* headlined its coverage, "Ohio Provides Lightning for Thunder."

Ohio basketball is a page out of "Family Ties." Take the Etheridges. Recent all-stater Todd, his brothers Steve and Scott, his father David, and his uncle Mike are among the school's all-time 12 top scorers. Two sisters, including Jennifer who averaged 13.3 points per game for the Lady Bulldogs in 1986–87, and two other uncles have also played for Ohio. In addition, there were three Dorans on the legendary 1985–86 boys' team and three Duffy sisters on the girls' squad two seasons later. Current star Jody Harris is playing in the spirit of brother Lance, the school's second all-time career scorer with 1,936 points, and grandfather W.C. Anderson, who amassed 755 in 1943–44.

While the Bureau communities have so far rejected consolidation, they are likely to embrace the "cooperative" concept, whereby two schools field a joint athletic team or one will conduct a special academic course open to both. Neponset, which plays games at "big city" Kewanee and has a senior class of six, is already in this bag.

Consolidation was an economic if not a quality necessity in most small-school areas, but the road hasn't been easy in Illinois. No one foresaw the breadth of the continuing exodus to the cities, a trend interrupted only in the seventies, and few expected the degree of resistance to consolidation that arose in certain enclaves. Illinois's most ambitious consolidation is probably at Stanford where eight onetime schools have been merged into Olympia High School. The enrollment, just under 700, is equal to the approximate population of the town. What used to be just plain "Oneida" is now expressed by the delightful acronym "ROWVA," a consolidation of Rio, Oneida, Wataga, Victoria, and Altona. "V.I.T." represents the consolidation of Vermont, Ipava, and Table Grove. "Broadlands ABL" represented the merger of Allerton, Broadlands, and Longview, but when Homer came in, the name was changed to "Heritage."

Hyphenations abound. There is M-V-K (Mazon-Verona-Kinsman), now to be joined by Seneca. There is M-D-R (Minonk-Dana-Rutland). These names may be awkward, but they retain community identity as opposed to such picturesque creations as Triopia, Century, Tri-Point, Hiawatha, Octavia, Egyptian, Shawnee, Jamaica, Shiloh, and River Ridge. The ultimate in hyphenation may have been dramatized by North Dakota's 1989 Class B football championship game: New England-Regent-Saint Mary's vs. Page-Hope-Clifford-Galesburg.

These are tough times for numerous Illinois school districts. Many are in financial difficulty, and school tax referendums don't pass easily. Under threats of partial closing, school bus cessation, and suspension of all student activities, including athletics, Lockport voters finally approved such a referendum in November 1989. It was the 11th try. Faced with the loss forever of a community symbol, Ohio and the other Bureau County villages have grit their teeth, reached into their pockets, and avoided all this. The Indian Valley Conference hangs in there, and Ohio keeps coming up with good players, often the brothers, sisters, sons, daughters, nieces, or nephews of former stars.

In 1947, armed with mighty plans for the future of education, Vernon Nickell, the state superintendent of public instruction, hoped that within 10 years all Illinois high schools would have enrollments of at least 200. It hasn't happened. It may never happen. Who knows how far the exodus will go?

CHARLIE'S ANGELS

Basketball success can be a major source of community pride. Conversely, continued failure can cause community malaise. This is the story of an ex-coach who left for greener pastures but whose heart never left the youngsters and community he had served. It's the story of renewal and rejuvenation in a town that sorely needed a lift. Coaching is an adventure at best, but, given a halfway normal environment, it can be rewarding in ways never quite understood in the outside world. You don't make much money, and you may take abuse from unknowledgeable people, but you're molding lives, not just teams. That's how the ex-coach looked at it. Let's join him in the midfifties.

Charlie Durham was at his FBI desk in Pittsburgh one March day in 1955 when the phone rang. Old friends had glorious news. Little Shawneetown High School had reached the Final Eight of the state tournament, upsetting suburban Rich Township, led by all-stater Roger Taylor and coached by the renowned Greg Sloan, before 7,000 spectators at Champaign.

It was an exhilarating experience. Charlie was far away now, but Shawneetown was still *his* team. In the three years ending in 1952, young Durham, just married and fresh out of college, had nursed the team in that faded, often flooded Ohio River town of 1,900 from a loser mentality to contendership, with pay dirt clearly in sight. The phrase "nowhere to go but up" never had a more classic application than in Shawneetown. When Durham arrived, its varsity hadn't won a game in years.

This was a town that progress had passed by. In the early nineteenth century when the river was queen, it was a gateway to the West, a bustling crossroads for steamboats, a stop on the Marquis de Lafayette's American tour, and a banking center that, regional historians contend, once refused a $1,000 loan to the infant, unproven city of Chicago. A century later the Great Flood of 1937 so ravaged the town that most of the populace was finally moved to higher ground three miles from the treacherous river. This created two entities, Old Shawneetown and New Shawneetown, with major economic problems remaining. Where river pirates, keelboaters, fur trappers, and salt miners once cavorted, there was little now stirring.

By reinstilling pride, emphasizing fundamentals, and coordinating closely with junior high coach Barney Genisio, Durham had turned the basketball program around. Now, three years later in a faraway city where new opportunity had beckoned, he pondered the old town's success that had finally come under successor Genisio. A host of memories from the early slogging days flashed through his mind.

There was the fine teamwork eventually achieved by an integrated squad in "border country". . .eating hamburgers on the bus with the black players, who weren't allowed in many restaurants, while another teacher accompanied the white players inside. . .the school and community pride finally forged. . .the evolution from half-filled gym to automatic sellout. . . the night their departing bus was stoned in Sturgis, Kentucky, after Shawneetown's predominantly black team had routed the locals by 33 points. . .

Just a few weeks before school opening in 1949, Durham inspected the gym. It was a "junk yard" and a shock. He spent hours cleaning, stacking, and trashing, then psyched up to call on the principal, also new. He told him he planned to visit each member of the school board—that evening. To each he said it was no wonder that the team was the perennial conference doormat and that students were known elsewhere as "river rats." He invited each to inspect the huge pile of junk, including old metal lockers, that he wanted to be hauled away. If the board members didn't want a change, he didn't want the job. But if they did, he promised that cooperation, a few years' patience, and a small capital outlay could "turn things around."

After a few more days' work alone in the gym, the young coach had it neat enough for school opening. Then, at the eleventh hour, he received notice to appear before the board. He was apprehensive at this, guessing that the members planned to tell him in effect, "Thanks, kid, but your plans are a little ambitious for our pocketbooks; our economic problems extend a little beyond basketball, and we've decided to hire someone else." But no. They'd searched their souls, decided they had a stake in all the school's activities, gave Durham approval to purchase gym mats as well as new lockers for 10 players, and promised him new uniforms the following year.

The first meeting with his players was Shock Number 2. The boys looked unkempt and forlorn. Their heads were always bowed. Knowing that most of them were poor and/or had farm chores to perform mornings and evenings, Durham expressed sympathy for personal problems and promised an open-door policy, always in strictest confidence. He also talked about self-worth, personal pride, and general appearance. Hereafter whenever they showed up for a game, either at home or to board the bus for an away game, they were to have neat, combed hair, shirt and tie, and shined shoes. He knew that several of them didn't own suits. The youngsters obeyed Durham's dicta to the letter, except that for the first game some of them appeared with ties in hand. They asked the coach to do the tying for them. No one in their families knew how.

On the technical side it was fundamentals, fundamentals, fundamentals. As an antidote to the "line drives" he found two of his players shooting, Durham asked the lads to stretch a string two feet above and four feet in front of the outdoor goal. Thus they learned "soft touch."

In the first season Shawneetown won 1 game out of 20—against weak Mill Shoals. The papers made quite a fuss. The drought was over. All of a sudden it seemed that every student was holding his or her head a little higher. But 1 game does not a program make. A long road lay ahead.

In the second season the Indians won 11 games, including 3 in tournaments, and the frosh-sophs (Papooses) posted a 13-7 record. Excitement started mounting around town, and, for the first time in years, spectators had to worry about getting a seat. There was vibrancy and just a little expectation at all levels—varsity, frosh-soph, and junior high.

In the third season the varsity finished at .500, but the real story was an outstanding contingent of freshmen on a 16-4 frosh-soph squad. The most promising were guard Garrison Newsom and center Bobby Spottsville who, along with forward Jack Nolen, would three years later fashion a 32-0 pre-Champaign record and engineer the school's only "Sweet 16" appearance in 82 years. They were the last and best of Charlie's boys.

Shawneetown had only one day to savor its 65-60 victory over Rich. It fell a 66-48 victim in the quarterfinals to Princeton, led by Joe Ruklick, who became Northwestern University's all-time scoring leader and a Philadelphia Warrior in the NBA. But with Charlie Durham the point was made. His freshmen had carried the "river rats" on the final leg from Zerosville to 32-1. He walked a little taller just thinking about it.

THE GIRLS WERE FIRST

*Careful research explodes myths and uncovers wholly
unexpected facts. Girls' basketball in Illinois didn't
start in 1975–76, the first season of IHSA tournament
sponsorship. Nor did girls just follow the boys in the
early years. They came first—in 1895. Eleven years
later, in the stated belief that basketball was "too unladylike" and "too exhausting," the IHSA abolished girls'
competition among member schools. Did the powers
really believe their rhetoric, or was this an economic
measure in disguise? Let Scott Johnson of Mahomet,
Illinois, a meticulous researcher and editor of* Illinois
High School Sports Historian, *tell the story.*

Perhaps the saddest aspect of my research into the early years of high
school basketball in the Chicago area was the discovery that schoolgirls
had a full-fledged basketball program, equal to the boys', that was destroyed
by the Victorian attitudes of parents and educators. The girls of the late
1890s and early 1900s were not merely hangers-on; they were pioneers
of the sport of basketball, rewriting high school sports policy with each
season. Girls played the first high school basketball games in Illinois,
formed the state's first prep basketball league, participated in intersectional
and interstate contests, and generally behaved like boys. Ultimately, that
was their undoing.

When it was introduced into the girls' athletic program in 1895, basketball was an immediate and welcome remedy for the boredom of the cal-
isthenics that were popular at the end of the last century. Out went the
Indian clubs, dumbbells, ladders, and wooden horses; in came the bloomers
and basketball hoops. Since the rules encouraged action and strategy but
specifically discouraged rough play, physical education instructors were
not reluctant to let the girls give the game a try. It would be a vast understatement to say that girls were enthusiastic about the new game; in fact,
basketball became the most popular sport for girls practically overnight.

The first high school basketball teams in Illinois were teams of girls.
At least three were organized in 1895, at Austin, Englewood, and Oak Park.

These teams, along with squads from the University of Chicago, Lake Forest College, and Hull House, formed the nucleus of the new sport of women's basketball in Chicago. Almost immediately, the competitive urge brought these teams together on the court. After accepting a challenge from Austin, the girls of Oak Park High School practiced against boys' teams in anticipation of the match. Austin won the history-making contest, 16–4, on December 18, 1896, at Library Hall in Austin. The two teams played three more games that winter, with the series ending tied at two games apiece.

In 1900, high school basketball took its first big step on the way to becoming a major sport, and once again it was the girls who set the precedent. Managers of four high school teams — Austin, Englewood, Hyde Park, and West Division (later McKinley) — formed the Cook County Basketball League. Playing on Friday and Saturday nights throughout the winter, the girls completed a double round-robin schedule, won by Englewood in a play-off over Austin.

In the winter of 1902, the teams of the high school league split over whether to continue playing by interference (boys') rules and as a result no league was organized. The next year, the interference teams (Englewood, Hyde Park, Lake High, and South Chicago) resurrected the league, while the dissenters (Calumet, Lake View, Oak Park, and West Division) played free-lance games. Eventually, these differences were reconciled, and by 1905, 11 girls' teams, a new high, started the league season using the interference rules.

There were storm clouds looming on the horizon, however. When the girls set about to organize their league in 1906, Superintendent of Schools Edwin G. Cooley and several principals came out strongly against the move. They thought the long series of games needed to decide a championship was too exhausting for the girls. Despite this recommendation, the managers defiantly organized the league, and official resistance was postponed for another year. The authorities had given due warning, however: the 1906 season was to be the last hurrah for girls' basketball in Chicago.

The girls remained undaunted in the face of this injunction and continued to set important new precedents. A team from Phillips High School traveled to St. Joseph, Michigan, to become one of the first Illinois high school teams to leave the state. Then, at the end of the season, the league champions from Oak Park traveled to Springfield and St. Louis in the first basketball barnstorming tour by an Illinois high school team. The school board was not impressed or amused by this eleventh-hour attempt at promoting the goodwill of the sport. Superintendent Cooley could not be dissuaded, and there was no girls' basketball league in 1907. A few teams played random games, but without a championship to strive for, the exercise seemed futile.

On November 2, 1907, the Illinois High School Athletic Association ruled that interscholastic basketball contests between girls would not be allowed among its member schools. At the time, there were 300 high schools with girls' teams under the association's jurisdiction. The ruling did not affect the Chicago schools, which were not members, but its chilling effect was felt in the city as well. In making its decision, the IHSAA concluded that "the game is altogether too masculine and has met with much opposition on the part of parents. The committee finds that roughness is not foreign to the game, and that the exercise in public is immodest and not altogether ladylike." Schoolgirls were permitted to compete in intramural contests, but only if the gymnasium was guarded against the eager eye of masculine enthusiasts.

The IHSAA was far ahead of its time in banning girls' sports, which survived in most states until the late 1920s. But in Illinois, the joys of interscholastic basketball were for boys only from 1907 to 1973.

ECHOES FROM
THE NATIONALS

Yes, class, there was a national high school basketball tournament. It was big, it spanned the Roaring Twenties, and it was held in Chicago. This story resurrects some of its highlights and lore, supplementing them with the memories of Toney Roskie, a distinguished Illinois prep coach who played on Rockford's 1923 runner-up team.

It was an idea whose time had come: a national high school basketball tournament. A national laboratory-clinic for coaches from the far corners of the land. A vehicle for studying the widely varying styles and techniques of a relatively new sport sorely needing uniformity in rules interpretation. An educational experience and an exercise in sportsmanship for youngsters in an era when travel was a luxury and provincialism was the norm.

The tourney would exist for 12 years, attract at its zenith as many as 43 teams, including 34 state champions, and be worthy of the name "National." It started in 1917, with the final buzzer sounding almost simultaneously with America's entrance into World War I. After a 2-year hiatus it resumed in 1920, lasting through 1930.

The site was the University of Chicago, then the scourge of the Big 10 in all sports and already known for a national interscholastic track and field meet originating in 1905. The architect was H.O. "Pat" Page, later a Basketball Hall of Fame electee who was then assistant to Chicago athletic director Amos Alonzo Stagg, the Grand Old Man of football. The event became popularly known as "the Stagg tournament." A subsequent director was H.O. "Fritz" Crisler, who would become football coach at the University of Michigan.

The first final was all-Illinois. Evanston, led by Chuck Carney, won in overtime from Freeport, led by Chester Weiderquist. Carney became an all-America football end and an all-Big 10 basketball center at the University of Illinois. Weiderquist was to be an all-America tackle at Washington & Jefferson.

Before the tournament had run its course, the state of Illinois would produce one more champion, Morton of Cicero (1927), and two more runners-up, Rockford (1923) and Canton (1928). Neighbor Indiana would claim a champion in Wingate (1920) and two runners-up, Crawfordsville (1920) and West Lafayette (1921). Neighbor Kentucky captured two titles, Lexington (1922) and Ashland (1928, the year little Carr Creek reached the quarterfinals and won hearts from coast to coast). National winner Morton of '27 hadn't even qualified for Illinois's state tournament. To fill out the draw it was admitted as representative of the strong Suburban League.

In an effort to provide the best possible clinical proving ground, officials made certain that first-round pairings would not pit teams from the same area against each other. The 40-team 1923 field included 27 state champions, 6 state runners-up, 1 interstate champion, 1 AAU titlist, 1 district champion, 1 city champion, 1 interstate runner-up, 1 city runner-up, and 1 state semifinalist.

Toney Roskie, known to later generations as coach at Todd School in Woodstock, Illinois, and program director at the school's summer camp in Michigan, was a regular forward on the Rockford team. Now 84, he remembers the big games in detail. En route to the national final Rockford defeated Pine Bluff (Arkansas), 35–17; Toledo Scott (Ohio), 34–28; Kansas City Westport (Missouri), 26–24; and Charleston (South Carolina), 45–21. At that point the honeymoon was over. The Rabs were dealt a severe lesson in the finale by North High of Kansas City, Kansas, 43–21.

In the Illinois semifinal Roskie and mates had eliminated Greenville's best team ever, 36–23, then were upset by little Villa Grove, 32–29. When Villa Grove was unable to accept the National Interscholastic invitation, Rockford stepped into the breach. Brace yourself for the Rabs' district (no regional in those days) and sectional victory scores that season: New Milford, 82–8; Genoa, 88–2; Dixon, 43–8; Rochelle, 54–11; Streator, 41–12; New Trier, 18–13; and Joliet, 15–10.

Rockford's only regular-season losses were at the hands of Freeport, 35–31, and the Alumni, 33–31, a Christmas holiday contest that wouldn't be counted today. Roskie and mates finished the season with a record of 27–4. The biggest "name" on the roster was left guard Bob Reitsch, later an all-America football lineman at Illinois. Roskie, the left forward, became a three-sport man at Lake Forest College, excelling in basketball and football. Other regulars were right forward Louis Behr, center Harold Gleichman, and right guard Clifford Nelson, who made all-national tournament.

Then the only public high school in a city of 80,000, Rockford had been a constant state tournament contender. Its 1919–23 credentials included one championship (1919), two runner-up finishes (1921 and 1923), one third place (1922), and one round-of-eight berth (1920).

Toney Roskie became one of that wonderful army of charismatic coaches who, in a simpler era, molded men while practicing psychology and public relations as effectively as any specialists in the Brave New World to come. It was said of him that he never lost enthusiasm and that he always seemed to know when to blow off steam and when to restrain.

Roskie recalls the class with which the National Interscholastic was staged and the genuine honor players felt in participating. The lads were treated like kings. They stayed at fraternity houses where it was almost "rush week," the members no doubt hoping to land a few of the guests for the old U of C. Tours of the city and a banquet on arrival night were on the schedule. Sportsmanship and personal dedication were real commodities at the national prep events. When members of the 1927 Huron, South Dakota, team read that Florence, Mississippi, home of their conquerors in the third-place play-off, had been hard hit by a flood, they spearheaded a fund drive. A $1,000 check was sent by Huron to the town of Florence "in appreciation of our association on the basketball floor." When his hometown, Georgetown, Texas, was swept by floods and was unable to pay his railroad fare, the state 100-yard dash champion rode the rods to Chicago and placed.

H.K. Long, coach of Morton's '27 champions, recalled that when players shook hands with fouled-out opponents, the gestures seemed genuine. Losing team members would go to the winners' locker room to wish them well.

While Roskie's 1923 team was tall for the times, averaging 6 feet, Morton won with a starting five averaging 5-8½ and 146 pounds. Much of its offense was based on stalling. It sought an early lead, then 5-7 guard Michael Rondinella would hold the ball until the opposition forced the issue. Thereupon he would drive around his defender or screen for a teammate who would drive or feed.

In the beginning, the National Interscholastic was a "must" for coaches. It was a vehicle for keeping up. Those who couldn't attend read the coverage and studied the play diagrams in the coaching magazine *Athletic Journal*. As with all promotions, however, the event eventually came under criticism. Although facts proved otherwise, some felt that the University of Chicago was unfairly profiting from the sponsorship. The National Federation of State High School Associations, which Stagg had fostered and helped create, was becoming stronger each year and began to look askance at privately sponsored events involving member schools. Administrators worried about extra time away from school: the nationals required successful teams to play five or six games in five days. Basketball had progressed mightily since 1917, and the laboratory aspect of the tournament was not as compelling as formerly. Finally, the state tournaments were becoming more and more feverish. They, too, were time-takers, and by the time a champion had been determined, players, coaches, and fans were emotionally drained. After the big state trophy, what else was worth fighting for? How could a team get up again?

Mr. Stagg's National Interscholastic died after the 1930 competition. It was an idea whose time had gone.

TOWN IN MOURNING

Air tragedy had struck teams in other sports—the Wichita, Marshall, and Cal Poly football teams, the U.S. boxers and skaters, the Manchester United soccer squad—and on Tuesday night, December 13, 1977, it struck a basketball team. A chartered plane carrying 14 University of Evansville players, the coach, the trainer, two managers, two publicity men, a sportscaster, the university controller, two fans, and a five-man crew crashed in rain and heavy fog shortly after takeoff from the local airport. There were no survivors. Seven of the players, including Illinois all-stater Mike Duff, were freshmen, just six months out of high school. Duff was one of two victims from Eldorado, Illinois, population 4,800. Here Pulitzer Prize winner Tom Fitzpatrick of the Chicago Sun-Times *reports from the joint funeral services held in the high school gym and attended by 3,000 people. The verses are from A.E. Housman's "To an Athlete Dying Young."*

The time you won your town the race
We chaired you through the market place;
Man and boy stood cheering by,
And home we brought you shoulder high.

Lou Beck closed his drugstore so he could go to the funeral. So did every other merchant in town.

It was a bright, sunny day and unseasonably warm. Because so many persons were going to the services for Mike Duff, 18, and Kevin Kingston, 21, some decided to walk to the gymnasium rather than get caught in the overcrowded high school parking lot.

Beck's wife, Pann, arrived at Eldorado High School more than an hour early. She is the best piano player in town, and it was her job to play while the mourners entered the gym.

Everybody in town knows that Pann plays beautifully. But they kept whispering to one another that they'd never heard her play so softly or with such feeling before.

Shortly before the service began, Bob Brown, a big, burly man who had coached Kevin and Mike in high school, led an entourage into the gym where they had known such glory.

Following Brown were two dozen young men, all wearing purple jackets, who had played either basketball or football with the two young men who had died with the University of Evansville basketball team in a plane crash Tuesday night.

Brown looked around the gym. He spotted the floral arrangements with real basketballs set into them. Then he saw the two gunmetal-gray caskets.

Brown pulled a handkerchief from his pocket and covered his face. Then he slumped into his chair. Not once during the service that followed did he remove the handkerchief from his face.

> *Today the road all runners come,*
> *Shoulder-high we bring you home*
> *And set you at your threshold down,*
> *Townsman of a stiller town.*

After Brown entered, six young men who had been Kingston's teammates the year he was captain walked in through the same tunnel they used as players and took seats near Kingston's casket.

Following them, six more young men who had been Duff's teammates the year he was captain entered by the same route and took seats by Duff's casket.

Kingston's parents entered next. Don Kingston, 46, is a history teacher at the school. For years he has also been assistant basketball and football coach. He walked in holding hands with his wife, Wanda.

Walking with them was Kevin's sister, Valery, who is a cheerleader at the school.

"She's really a strong girl," someone whispered. "She hasn't missed a day of school since it happened. She doesn't talk to anyone, but she hasn't missed a class."

George Lewis, 30, a reporter for the local paper, remembered how Don had found out about the plane crash.

"We were both over to Norris City, where Eldorado played Tuesday night," Lewis said. "I was driving on the highway right behind Don. I heard on the car radio a news flash about the Evansville team's plane crashing and that maybe there were no survivors. I thought maybe Don had been listening to that station, too.

"When we got back to town, we both parked at the high school. Don got out of the car, and he just came up to me and hugged me. He said, 'O, my God.' I realized then that Don had been listening to the same newscast."

Friday afternoon Don Kingston's head was held high.

"He's amazing," Lewis said. "At the funeral home last night he told me he realizes he has to look ahead. He's going to keep right on going to all the basketball games he can.

" 'The stars are made out there on that floor,' he told me, 'and I want to see them.' "

Eyes the shady night has shut
Cannot see the record cut,
And silence sounds no worse than cheers
After earth has stopped the ears.

It was estimated that 5,000 persons passed through the funeral home Thursday night. There were more than 3,000 in the gymnasium for the funeral.

Mike Duff's family were the next to enter.

Mike's mother, Kay, was accompanied by her husband, Dr. John Barrow. Following her were Mike's sisters, Mary Jane, 14, and Rita, 16, as well as Mike's girlfriend, Sherry Boggess, 17.

At the funeral home Mike's mother had walked up to Lewis and hugged him. "I always used to kid you about your old camera," she said, "and tell you it looked like a lunchbox. Now I've got to thank you, because those pictures you gave me are all I have left of Mike."

By the time the services began, it seemed that everyone in town was inside the gym.

Owen Brill, 40, who had covered every game that Mike and Kevin had played in high school, was there. Brill had talked about those games earlier.

"I remember I nicknamed Kevin 'The Bandit,' because he was so good at stealing the ball from enemy players," he said.

"I remember Mike slam-dunking the ball or swishing long shots with such a high arc. I'll always remember Mike as a gentle giant who was worshiped by every fan.

"I remember the night he tore up his knee in a football game at West Frankfort, and I remember how disconsolate he was the night he sprained an ankle at Benton.

"He looked up from the trainer's table and asked, 'Owen, what else can happen to me?' "

Smart lad, to slip betimes away
From fields where glory does not stay,
And early though the laurel grows,
It withers quicker than the rose.

Mike Duff was 6 feet 7 inches tall and weighed 215 pounds. Two months ago he had filled out a publicity form at the University of Evansville, telling a little about his likes and dislikes.

"My inspiration has always been Coach Bob Brown," Duff wrote, "because he knows so much about basketball. . . . My favorite professional athlete is Bill Walton. I have never had a bigger thrill in sports than going to play in the Illinois state tournament."

Duff had gone there three times and made all-state twice. College coaches who had seen him play tabbed him as a sure pro prospect.

The ceremony began with the Phelps Brothers, a gospel quartet, singing, "Oh, What a Sunrise." Toward the end of the song came the words, "Death will take us, but only to sleep in the arms of our Saviour."

The first clergyman to speak was the Reverend Joseph Lawler of nearby Ridgway. "Young people are always looking for heroes," Father Lawler said, "and in Mike and Kevin they found two heroes who were eminently worthy."

The Reverend Clyde Grogan, a huge, bearded man in a black sweater, spoke next, saying, "We are not here because Mike and Kevin died but because they have lived. They've been part of us. They've helped us to laugh, to cheer, to enjoy life. We are here to say thanks, Mike, and thanks, Kevin. Thank you for living and helping us to live, too."

As Father Grogan spoke, mourners all over the gymnasium, perhaps recalling the times they had seen the two young men demonstrate their remarkable athletic skills, began dabbing at their eyes.

Kingston, three years older than Mike, also had filled out a publicity form at Evansville.

He was 6 feet 2 and weighed 170 pounds. He had been co-captain of both the basketball and football teams in high school and had run the half-mile on the track team.

The 1974 basketball team which Kingston captained was ranked Number 1 in Illinois Class A all season long. It won 24 straight before losing in its final tournament game.

Kingston said his idol was his dad, Don, whom he described as a great teacher and coach who stood behind him in everything he did.

His one gripe, Kevin wrote, was people who kept saying he'd never make it as a college player. The biggest thrill of his life was being granted a basketball scholarship in his senior year after starting collegiate athletics as a walk-on.

> Now you will not swell the rout
> Of lads that wore their honours out,
> Runners whom renown outran
> And name did die before the man.

The last of the three clergymen to speak was the Reverend Bill Tamberlin of the First Baptist Church in Eldorado.

"The tragedy is great," Mr. Tamberlin said, "and though we accept what's happened, we don't understand it."

The two caskets were lifted off their racks and gently placed into two waiting hearses by the young athletes.

Then they turned to Coach Brown. Without thinking, all 12 moved toward Brown and hugged him just as they used to do after winning a big game.

There is no way to describe the emotion of that moment.

Reprinted from Tom Fitzpatrick, "Farewell to Kevin and Mike," *Chicago Sun-Times*, December 17, 1977. © With permission of Chicago Sun-Times, Inc., 1989.

ILLINOIS POTPOURRI

Superlatives, oddities, and memorable anecdotes from Illinois, collected over the years.

The old Brussels gym sweats when the humidity is high. Visiting rival Hardin Calhoun was leading Brussels, 40–22, at halftime in December 1989, but players were slipping all over the floor. A packed house of about 350 fans didn't help conditions. Brussels officials had three alternatives. They could call the game. They could play the second half at a later date. Or they could play the the second half right away—at Hardin Calhoun 16 miles away.

Because of the rivalry aspect, they opted for Number 3. Most of the spectators made the trip down two-lane County Route 1. The headlight procession was reminiscent of a scene in *Hoosiers*. Brussels (enrollment 67) lost to Hardin Calhoun (enrollment 130), 83–59, but ingenuity and the fans' love of the game transcended all.

They called Mel Stuessy "the coach who couldn't lose." It was wartime, and the date was February 24, 1944. The event was the district tournament final, and Stuessy found himself coaching both teams. He had coached one of them, St. Mary's of Woodstock, for years. When Hebron, 11 miles up Highway 47, lost its coach, Superintendent Paul Tigard asked Stuessy if he would handle things at his school as well. Stuessy accepted, arranged schedules and practice sessions so they wouldn't conflict, and guided both schools to winning seasons.

When Fate finally put the two teams on the floor at the same time—and against each other—Stuessy remained with St. Mary's, his original school. He asked Superintendent Tigard to sit on the Hebron bench and handle changes. St. Mary's won the game, 33–30, and advanced to the regional.

Stuessy, basically a football man, was in the awning business in Woodstock. He took the St. Mary's job on a handshake, receiving a check from the parishioners at the end of the year. St. Mary's was closed in 1959, replaced by Marian Central Catholic, a countywide institution.

They don't make 'em like Arthur Trout any more. All coaches are of necessity taskmasters, coordinators, motivators, philosophers, counselors, and PR men, and even today many of them teach subjects other than PE or driver education. But Trout added extra dimensions in his 37 years at Centralia High. He injected scholarship into coaching. He stood for ideals in dramatic ways. He posted a long-standing national record of 809 victories at a single school. He produced a parade of stars, including Dike Eddleman, Lowell Spurgeon, John Scott, Fred Schlichtman, Ken McBride, Colin Anderson, Sam Mooney, and Harry Blakely. He wrote florid prose, and his occasional eccentricities delighted the media.

Trout started coaching in the 1914–15 season when the gym was in the basement of the school building, the backboard surfaces were not uniform, the ceiling was only two feet above the backboard tops, and long before free substitution, the 10-second and 3-second rules, and abolition of the automatic center jump after each basket. Those were days of slick floors, wood-burning stoves close by, and walls for court boundaries.

Trout stories are legion.

As an object lesson during the Wonder Five season of 1940–41, he alternated two teams at powerful Taylorville—all-stater Eddleman with four reserves and the other four regulars without Eddleman. This conveyed a message of mutual need while virtually engineering the team's only defeat in a 44-game string.

When he had 10 players of reasonably even ability in 1942–43, he alternated two teams, calling one the "A's," the other the "Alphas."

When his lone black player was told he would have "to eat outside" as the team assembled for lunch at an upstate restaurant, Trout commanded his troops to leave the premises, admonishing management that "the Civil War is over and the slaves have been freed." When a referee made a racial remark to one of his black players, he whisked the team off the floor, insisting that the principles of human dignity overrode the threat of punishment by the IHSA.

He taught the long, high-arch, two-hand "eye shot" (the media liked the term "kiss shot" better). The idea was just to hit the rim, but how beautifully those shots often swished. He relished the perception his team's nickname, "Orphans," conveyed to fans outside southern Illinois. Centralia was not a small, downtrodden school; it was the largest in its area.

Old-timers recall a time or times when Trout took special action to stop fan abusiveness toward the officials. He grabbed the mike, strode to the center of the floor, halted play, and made an announcement. He said he had hired the officials because they had good credentials, and he was ashamed of the crowd's treatment of them. He decreed that there would be no further booing or other actions of disrespect. Those unable to comply could collect refunds at the ticket office.

Trout combined game trips with educational touches. In line with his calling as a civics and economics teacher and when train schedules permitted, he would take his players to the local courthouse. With luck a trial would be in progress, and what more practical reflection of life for a civics student?

After a football game at Wheaton, he stayed overnight in order to shepherd his players to Chicago's Art Institute the following day, there to conduct a lecture on the masterpieces and their creators.

He had a battery of biblical and Latin expressions for game developments and locker room communication. They ranged from old-fashioned chewing out to scholarly lectures and bended-knee pleas for compliance. Once he burst into the locker room singing a parody on a tune from "Oklahoma" that went something like this:

> *All the Orphans are standing like statues.*
> *All the Orphans are standing like statues.*
> *The crap is as high*
> *As an elephant's eye*
> *And it looks like it's growing way up to the sky.*
> *O, what a disastrous evening,*
> *O, what a disastrous day...*
> *I've got a disastrous feeling*
> *You'll never be able to play.*

They did though. Mr. Trout was one of a kind.

Retired now from a long successful career as coach at Galesburg, Gerald Phillips was driving as a spectator to the 1955 state tournament in Champaign. Alone with his memories, he pitted his best teams against each other in fantasy games. His favorite was the gang of 1945 that lost an overtime cliffhanger to eventual champion Decatur, 73-72, in the quarterfinals. What a game! The lead changed hands 33 times, including 6 times during the overtime. Galesburg's Evans, Barstow, and Graham against Decatur's Doster, Riley, and Rutherford! An astronomical score for that era and a game on every old-timer's "most thrilling" list. Suddenly there it was—on the radio..."Graham's free throw puts Galesburg ahead by one...Riley's bucket puts Decatur back in the lead...Evans hits, but Riley counters again...Rutherford and Graham trade free throws...Barstow scores from the side to put Galesburg up by 1...just two seconds to go and Doster tips one in...Decatur wins by 1!" The agony ended, but how could this be? Was it a time warp? A dream? Phillips pulled off the road and tried to relax. Then the announcer explained. This was Decatur territory, and radio station WSOY was saluting a past local achievement shortly before a new Decatur team would take the floor in Champaign. Phillips sighed and resumed his journey. The old classics never die.

It was halftime at a charity game before 20,000 Chicago Stadium fans in October 1985, and Magic Johnson, Michael Jordan, Isiah Thomas, Dominique Wilkins, Mark Aguirre, and the rest gathered around a local cab driver to pay their respects. The cabbie was Nate "Sweetwater" Clifton, who went from DuSable High School to the Globetrotters in the early forties, then, past his prime, became the second (by minutes) black to enter the NBA. "He took abuse for less than $7,500 a year so you can go out and earn a million today," the Reverend Jesse Jackson told the superstars.

Not all stories have upbeat endings. During the 1945–46 season Dale White of Irving, a tiny three-year high school in Montgomery County, piled up an incredible 1,029 points, 60 more than the seemingly unbreakable 969 posted by Centralia's Dike Eddleman in 1940–41. In the waning days of its existence, Irving had perpetrated such massacres as 133–14 over Harvel, 112–18 over Marine, 106–17 over Rockbridge, 102–53 over Oconee, and 98–22 over Panama, all during a 44-day period early in 1946.

Julius Podshadley, Irving's coach, principal, and math teacher, said he ran up the score only on teams that had done so on Irving in the past, a declaration suggesting the direst of possible pasts.

Dale was a media darling. He gave district schools a special place in the sun although none of his three teams was able to win a district tournament. When he received an "outstanding high school athlete" award in a faraway place, all the little Davids seemed to share the joy. Critics debated whether Dale's 1,029 points should be recognized as a state record. Liberals said, "A high school is a high school; give the kid his record." Conservatives countered, "A schedule full of three-year schools can't be compared with one comprising four-year schools exclusively. How about games with two-year schools [there were a few in those days]? Would you count them?"

Dale enrolled at Hillsboro, the "big school" six miles down Highway 16, for his senior year. Coached by Joe Fearheiley, Hillsboro was a year away from a "Sweet 16" appearance and building up to perhaps its greatest team in history, the Ott-Boston-Wallace-Sturgeon-Demas juggernaut that was state runner-up in 1949. It would be a fairy story ending if Dale had been part of at least the beginning of all this, but he wasn't. He was on the squad at Hillsboro but saw limited action. A much storied scorer didn't crack the lineup at the "big school."

Any time a sophomore substitute, on the floor for only 40 seconds, rattles in a three-pointer in a second overtime to win a game before a packed house, it's at least temporary local news. But what Patrick Lyerla of Worden did against Mt. Olive on February 18, 1988, carried much more significance.

It broke the team's 49-game losing streak that had run since January 11, 1986. In addition, this was the final home game ever for 63-student Worden High School, scheduled to be consolidated with Edwardsville five months later.

"Packed" stands in Worden meant a crowd of 500. Alumni, former players, and townspeople who had never showed up during the long drought were on hand—to say farewell to the old school and hope against hope for a happy ending. Lyerla's shot was reminiscent of the perils of Pauline. With hearts riding on it, the ball hit the backboard, bounced off the front of the rim, then up, down, and in. Coach Steve Ondes waited for something to go wrong. It always did before. But not this time. Worden had finally won a game—in its last possible home try.

They called it "Chuck Keller's Revenge." In 1979 Mr. Keller, an Effingham oilman, had brought the German giant, Uwe Blab, to Effingham where he helped the local school to the state AA final as a junior and the Final Eight as a senior. Disappointed that Uwe chose Indiana University over the University of Illinois, Keller became instrumental in bringing two other German phenoms to the state but not to Effingham. Jens Kujawa, later the regular center at Illinois, and Olaf Blab, Uwe's younger brother, wound up with conference rivals Taylorville and Charleston, respectively!

The Saga of Jasper Robinson during the 1962–63 season almost upstaged the whole of statewide competition. Robinson was an all-state forward on a highly regarded Rockford Auburn team coached by the legendary Dolph Stanley. The problem was his questionable birth date. Was he or wasn't he eligible?

Robinson's mangled birth certificate in Junction City, Arkansas, appeared to give the date as December 2, 1943, which put him on the wrong side of the IHSA's December 11 cutoff date. However, his father said he believed the date to be December 24, his service record so indicated, and it was said that if the certificate were held up to the light, a "4" imprint could be seen. The IHSA Board accepted the December 2 date as legitimate and declared Robinson ineligible.

A Rockford contingent journeyed to Arkansas in search of evidence, only to discover that fire had destroyed early school records and that there weren't any baptismal records. At the IHSA board's next regular meeting, Jasper's father testified, and affidavits from friends and relatives supported the belief that the youngster was born on December 24. However, the board upheld its original ruling. Jasper and his father then filed for an injunction in Winnebago County Circuit Court, barring the IHSA, its executive secretary, and the Rockford Board of Education from declaring the youngster ineligible. The injunction was granted and appealed.

Meanwhile Jasper was allowed to play, and he led the Auburn Knights into the "Sweet 16," handing the IHSA a hot potato of monumental proportions. What if Auburn should win the championship and then be declared irretrievably ineligible? Jasper scored 15 points as Auburn defeated Aledo, 62–51, in the Moline supersectional and advanced to the Final Eight at Champaign. There the bubble burst: Springfield Lanphier nipped the Knights, 58–56, and IHSA officials breathed a sigh of relief.

The Jasper Robinson case wasn't officially closed until December 31, 1963, when the IHSA's appeal was upheld. Auburn was forced to forfeit 15 victories.

In the early days, coaches tended to look upon shooting success as a "law of averages" thing. In 1916 Wayne Gill of Decatur sank 12 baskets in an afternoon game at Bloomington but was not used in a second contest scheduled that night. "He was so hot this afternoon I knew he wouldn't be able to hit a thing tonight," his coach said.

Bobby Plump's 4:13 ball-holding stint in the late stages of Milan's epic 1954 Indiana state championship effort has been chronicled far and wide. Not so storied is the 6:03 *dribbling* stall logged by Jim Lazenby of Pinckneyville in Illinois's 1955 third-place game. With opponent Princeton creeping up on the scoreboard, Pinckneyville got the tip at the start of the fourth quarter, and Lazenby dribbled for 2 minutes. The team then called time-out to give him a rest. Lazenby dribbled for another 3:29 before drawing a foul. He hit a free throw whereupon Pinckneyville, under rules of the day, took the ball out of bounds. Lazenby dribbled for another 34 seconds before being fouled again. Pinckneyville won, 58–53, in a game that may have inspired the five-second rule.

This was also the "year of the 6 points in 1 second." West Rockford met Elgin in the final. With his team behind 6 points with 2:19 to play, Nolden Gentry, West's all-state forward, hit a 20-footer and was fouled. Under a new rule providing for a bonus free throw on all fouls committed in the final 3 minutes, Gentry received two shots and made them both, cutting Elgin's lead to two. On Elgin's throw-in Rex Parker of West drew a charging foul and made both his free throws. The game had been tied in 1 second of elapsed time. Gentry tapped in a rebound in the final seconds for a 61–59 West Rockford victory and the state championship.

Who dares to rank the impacts of basketball upsets occurring decades apart? Most of Illinois's candidates belong to "the old days"—before the small schools had a tournament of their own and before there was as much intersectional play as there is today. Following in chronological order are the state's most shocking prep results within the author's 55-year memory:

1936—Decatur 26, Danville 22 (state final; Danville was 26–0 going in, Decatur 23–11)

1939—Indianola 28, Danville 22 (regional tournament; Danville was Big 12 co-champion; Indianola had 55 students)

1940—Lewistown 31, Hebron 30 (state tournament; Hebron had been a tourney favorite)

1941—Morton of Cicero 30, Centralia 29 (state tournament; Centralia, with a 43–1 record, had been considered a wonder team)

1946—Douglass of Mounds 55, West Frankfort 51 (regional tournament; West Frankfort had been Number 1, 2, or 3 in state rankings all season and owned the only victory over eventual state champion Champaign; Douglass lost decisively the next night)

1948—Marion 65, Collinsville 60 (state tournament; Collinsville, at 27–1 and led by all-stater Sammy Miranda, was the co-favorite; Marion, at 23–10, had a height average just over five-ten when using its center and just over five-nine when using a three-guard offense)

1951—Hinsdale 47, Morton of Cicero 46 OT (regional tournament; Morton, with three major college regulars-to-be, was unbeaten and ranked Number 1 in the state; Hinsdale, with nine losses, had upset unbeaten La Grange the night before)

1954—Mt. Vernon 76, DuSable of Chicago 70 (state final, the most chronicled game of them all)

1957—Marquette of Ottawa 79, Seneca 54 (regional tournament; Marquette brought in a record of 1–20 and just a week before had lost to Seneca, a team that had suffered only one defeat all season)

1976—Peoria Richwoods 85, Galesburg 79 OT and Chicago Weber 73, East Leyden 68 (regional finals; both Galesburg and East Leyden were unbeaten, top ranked, and eliminated on the same night)

For a twelfth upset, the mind wrestles between Urbana Uni High's once-in-a-lifetime victory over Urbana in a 1943 regional and Mt. Pulaski's triumph over Providence St. Mel of Chicago in the 1984 Class A state tourney.

Robin Nika and Les Lee were starry-eyed eight-year-old third graders when they first fantasized about winning the state tournament. Robin was white. His father, Bob Nika, was coach of the Lanphier High School team in Springfield, and he permitted his son and pal Les, who was black, to work out in the gym. They would conduct imaginary Lanphier games, always culminating in one or the other making a heroic shot in the "state final" as the waning seconds tolled "4-3-2-1. . ."

At various times through the years they reminded each other of the dream. By 1983 each was a regular on a strong 30–3 Lanphier team. Ten seconds away from a four-point victory over Peoria in the state AA championship game, they met at midcourt and exchanged knowing smiles.

"It all started in the third grade, and now it was really going to happen," said young Nika. "It was as if we'd been practicing eight years for this moment."

Disaster is the mother of legislation. Champaign, coached by Harry Combes, played most of its four "Sweet 16" games in 1945 with only 7 players. Rules at that time provided for 10-man squads with no replacements. Team captain Jim Cottrell came down with a strep throat before the tournament. Substitute center John McDermott broke a leg as he drove into a basket support during the team's opener. And guard Del Cantrell tore knee cartilage as he came down from the bleachers after the next game. Despite the problems, Champaign still reached the final, losing to Decatur, 60–54. Today Illinois state tourney qualifiers are permitted 12-player squads.

Girls' basketball in Illinois came of age on February 13, 1989—on the wings of a defeat rather than a victory. That was the night the state record 65-game winning streak of Maine West came to an end. Amid more fanfare ever seen or dreamed at any girls' game east of Iowa, the defending state Class AA champions from Des Plaines lost, 53–46, to perennial rival New Trier in a sectional semifinal on the Niles West floor in Skokie. The milestone of defeat focused a national spotlight on girls' prep basketball and told doubting Thomases just how far all women's athletics had come.

Anyone who has ever watched girls play a game after school before a crowd of 11, with no chance of even meager media coverage, or heard fans indict girls' competition as too strenuous or unladylike, or listened to complaints that "boring girls' sports" are cramping the athletic budget would have been spellbound by the atmosphere at Niles West. The stands were jammed with 3,600 spectators, and those arriving even 45 minutes early had to park more than five blocks from the gym. Two radio stations, all local TV stations, all Chicago-area daily newspapers, and several weeklies covered the spectacle.

The well-played game had all the conventional ingredients of a boys' tournament contest: sound play, the seesaw score, the big star in foul trouble, the dramatic three-pointer in the clutch, the impending upset, continuous screaming, jubilation, and tears. Old-timers sighed. Girls had come a long way since the bloomer days.

For several weeks the Maine West team had been in the eye of a whirlwind that transcended any single game. Letters of respect and wonder poured in from faraway people who had never before heard of Des Plaines, Illinois. A seemingly indestructible group of teenagers had done more for the advancement of women's athletics than any speech or legislation ever could.

As Dike Eddleman of Centralia is believed to be the only athlete ever to compete in the Olympics, Rose Bowl, and basketball all-star game, so there are only three known Illinois high school products whose names appear in the encyclopedias of all three major American team sports—basketball, football, and baseball. Two of them are the well-known George Halas, originally of Chicago Crane, and Paddy Driscoll, originally of Evanston. The third, not so well known, is Art Bramhall of Oak Park-River Forest.

Bramhall played several seasons of basketball with the Chicago Bruins in the early thirties, a season with the football Chicago Bears in 1931, and two baseball games with the Philadelphia Phillies in 1935. Bramhall had been a perennial high school athlete. He played so long for Oak Park-River Forest that he was surely one reason for enactment of the eight-semester eligibility rule. Prior to Bramhall's time, it was common for an athlete to complete the football season, drop out, then re-enroll the following September. Bramhall was finally declared ineligible by Oak Park-River Forest, then entered St. Mel of the Chicago Catholic League. This precipitated an incident. Loyola University authorities would not allow Art to play in their annual national Catholic tournament, a decision that caused St. Mel to withdraw its entry.

Steinmetz and Foreman played to a double tie in the Chicago Public League on January 31, 1935. The lightweights were still tied, 20–20, after one overtime so let it go at that. The heavyweights were deadlocked, 24–24, at the end of regulation time, and officials decided against an overtime, thus completing a decisionless day.

Moline's grand old Wharton Field House is to Midwest high school athletics as Fenway Park is to major league baseball. It's a landmark. Built in 1928 with seating capacity of 5,200, it was considered an architectural wonder and a model of project organization. Wharton's first game was played only 10 months after the land was acquired and the first bond sold.

When the bonds were paid off, the field house was deeded to the public school system. The structure was named for T.F. Wharton, a John Deere executive who superintended the fund-raising.

Sixtieth anniversary festivities on December 20, 1988, included three games—sophomore girls, varsity girls, and varsity boys—as well as appropriate ceremonies, a "family night" price structure that admitted an entire family for five dollars, and a booster club-sponsored hot dog supper (one dollar). Among those present were past Moline coaches Jack Foley, Herb Thompson, and Whitey Verstraete, a Moline all-stater in the fifties; and James Rosborough, who as a 16-year-old junior sank Wharton's first basket—on December 21, 1928.

"It was a two-handed set shot at the north basket from the east end of the free throw line," the 76-year-old retired tool company president recalled.

Both Moline and sister city Rock Island are high on the list of 52 Illinois high schools known to have amassed 1,000 or more basketball victories through the 1988–89 season. Rock Island is 14th with 1,214 in 89 years. Moline is 18th with 1,184 in 76 years. Amazingly only .008 separates the rivals. Moline's percentage is .649, Rock Island's .641. Almost as amazing is a statistic revealing that four Quad City schools—Moline, Rock Island, East Moline, and Rock Island Alleman—have made 43 "Sweet 16" appearances and reached the semifinals 15 times without winning a single state title. The law of averages is overdue.

When Senator Paul Broyles of Mt. Vernon introduced a resolution in the Illinois legislature commending his hometown basketball team for winning the 1949 state championship, he touched off a succession of speeches by various colleagues, each praising the team of his own community. The orgy ended when Senator Libonati of Chicago's West Side proposed that Senator Barr of Joliet introduce a resolution commending the team at Stateville Penitentiary.

Thereupon the elderly Barr, apparently dozing in his seat and oblivious to the proceedings, rose and replied: "I am sure that Senator Libonati has enough clients and constituents in the institution to frame the necessary resolution."

Steve Boer, a 6-2 Timothy Christian (Elmhurst) forward, suffered a deep head gash when a light fixture fell from its moorings during the third quarter of a game at Nazareth Academy, La Grange Park, on January 6, 1984. With Nazareth leading, 37–26, the game was suspended and rescheduled.

The first great black basketball player in Illinois was not Nate "Sweetwater" Clifton, DuSable '41, or John Scott, Centralia '37, or any of the Chicagoans of the thirties who became standouts on the Globetrotters or at all-black southern colleges. From the state tournament standpoint he was Lynch Conway, a forward on Peoria Central's 1908 champions. His 11 field goals remained a title-game record for 42 years. From the overall state standpoint the first great black was probably Sam Ransom of Hyde Park (Chicago). He led his teams to numerous championships: Cook County League basketball in 1901 in addition to two county titles in both football and baseball and a Number 1 national ranking in football. He became a basketball standout at Beloit College.

Bob Pligge was pursued by college even as a junior at Chicago's Taft High School where he averaged 23 points a game as a 6-1 guard in 1980–81. Bob was the most storied basketball player in Taft history, and his future looked eminently bright. Then in the summer his leg began hurting, and doctors advised some tests. There was malignancy. On October 16, shortly before the new Taft squad assembled, they amputated Bob's leg. There would be other dreams, but this one was over.

In the spirit of Jim Abbott, Monte Stratton, and Pete Gray, who have played major league baseball without one of their limbs, high school basketball can offer legions of courageous athletes who competed despite severe handicaps. The 1982–83 season revealed two memorable Illinois examples. Sebastian Borges, a regular at Von Steuben (Chicago), had been pronounced dead as a nine-year-old after he fell on a third rail at the Ravenswood L tracks. But someone at the hospital thought he could still be alive, and resuscitation revived him. They amputated his left arm up to the elbow. He persevered and years later made the Von Steuben varsity, averaging 10 points a game.

Seventeen miles west, in suburban Schaumburg, 6-7 senior Steve Courington had come to a crossroads. He had shown great promise as a sophomore, but now chemotherapy treatments in the wake of bone cancer had burned considerable muscle that couldn't be rehabilitated. Greatly weakened, Steve concluded that he could no longer contribute, turned in his uniform, and got on with his one-day-at-a-time life. So great was his inspiration to teammates that his name, by coach's order, remained on the gym scoreboard.

Another particularly doughty basketball player in Illinois annals is Jim Williams, who despite an artificial leg was a reserve center on Norris City's 1970–71 team. Jim wore a stocking over the limb, and some fans were not aware of his handicap. One day his coach, irked because his players had left the school bus dirty on a trip home, ordered them to run two punishment miles inside the gym. He forgot about Jim. When he looked up, there he was, running near the front. Jim never complained.

Unbeaten Lanark lost to Fulton, 63–57, in a Class A sectional final in 1973, but if it hadn't been for a favorable circuit court decision two and a half hours earlier, the team would have been disqualified from the tournament.

Under a little-known rule prohibiting a player from participating in two tournaments after February 10, the IHSA had disqualified Lanark, then five other schools, including two (Morrisonville and Cerro Gordo) that had already "won" Class A sectionals. The others were Bremen, a Class AA regional finalist against Thornton, and Petersburg Porta and Mason City, Class A sectional finalists against Carrollton and Bloomington Central Catholic, respectively. Each had allowed a sophomore player to compete in a frosh-soph tournament after the deadline date, then used him in a state tournament game.

Lanark appealed the IHSA decision to circuit court judge John W. Rapp in Mt. Carroll. He said that the association had no authority to impose the regulation. As a result, the IHSA, no doubt relieved that it wouldn't be required to order beaten teams into tournaments already postponed three days, reinstated the schools and life went on.

The best of the outstanding but unsung Xavier University (New Orleans) teams during the 1935–38 period were unique in that all five starters came from Chicago's Wendell Phillips High School. The players were Cleveland Bray, whose older brother, Agis, had led Phillips to the 1930 Chicago Public League heavyweight title before joining the Globetrotters; Leroy Rhodes; Tilford Cole; Charlie Gent; and William McQuitter. At one point Xavier's record was 67–2, and its two defeats were squeakers—33–32 to LeMoyne and 27–26 to Clark. Gant and McQuitter later coached in the Public League.

Illinois fans look wistfully on the Indiana-Kentucky all-star rivalry. They marvel at its staying power (it started in 1939), its competitiveness, and the substantial monies it has raised for the blind. They wish they had been first with the idea, and perhaps they can't be blamed for feeling that neighboring Corn Belt state Illinois would have been Indiana's more natural rival.

Old-timers point out that there *was* an Illinois-Indiana all-star game—on August 29, 1942, in Mt. Vernon, Illinois—and that the host state won, 36–30. Illinois's squad, featuring Dike Eddleman and Walt Kirk, later University of Illinois regulars, and Chuck Tourek, a Northwestern starter-to-be, was selected by a statewide vote of sportswriters. The Indiana squad included six members of the two-time state champion Washington Hatchets and three from Evansville Central's "best team ever," the only blemish on the Hatchets' 30–1 record during the 1941–42 season.

The game stemmed from a friendly argument between a coach, Paul Lostutter of Delphi, Indiana, and a former pupil, Doxie Moore, then coach at Mt. Vernon, Illinois. Lostutter would handle the Hoosier all-stars. Moore would organize the game, arrange civic festivities, and coach the Illinoisans. Besides Eddleman, Kirk, and Tourek, the Illinois squad comprised Don Morris, Earl Dodd, Jack Eadie, Joe Van Hoorweghe, Warren Collier, Galen Davis, and Gerald Dirksen. The Indiana squad included Jim Riffey, John Dejernett, Charles Harmon, Art Grove, Robert Donaldson, and Sid Raney, all of Washington, and Fred Althaus of Evansville Central.

The action was a classic example of how a well-oiled unit has an advantage over an all-star team with little experience in playing together, at least at the outset. The Hoosiers grabbed a 19–3 lead before the tide began to turn. Less than three minutes remained when Illinois finally took the lead. The game was a sellout, but the concept was short-lived. In November 1942 the Illinois High School Association banned all-star games not sanctioned by that body. The interstate contest was replaced by a North vs. South intrastate game in connection with a University of Illinois coaches' clinic. Even this experiment was brief. By 1947 it was history.

School was closed on the Monday following East St. Louis Lincoln's unprecedented third consecutive state AA championship in 1989, but it wasn't in tribute to the team. The poorly maintained sewers in this impoverished city backed up, flooding streets and stifling movement.

It isn't that the citizens of East St. Louis have become jaded by Lincoln's numerous boys' and girls' state basketball and track titles or the many state 6A state football championships won by rival East St. Louis Senior. Rather it's that the citizens can't allow themselves the luxuries of motorcades or gala communitywide celebrations. There was a basketball program at Lincoln during the 1989–90 season but to a great extent because angels provided money. The school board would have drastically cut the basketball budget, limiting travel to a 50-mile radius from the school. Coach Bennie Lewis, who produced four state AA championship teams in eight years, is used to tight budgets. He shelled out $200 of his own money during the 1989 Final Eight, because daily food allowances didn't allow his players much more than a single sandwich per meal.

The accomplishments of East St. Louis athletes never stand so tall as when arrayed against the socioeconomic environment. In the same metropolitan newspaper chronicling Lincoln's 1989 title effort was a story reporting that the city was nearly broke, that its employees were one payday behind, and that in the past they've gone as long as seven weeks without pay.

Wholesale counterfeiting of tickets cast a shadow over the 1924 Chicago city tournament at Loyola University. Regular admission was 50 cents, and bogus tickets were going for 35. Paid admissions totaled 2,100, but there were between 4,500 and 5,000 spectators inside. Students and outsiders were reported to be profiting to the tune of $50 a night, a mighty sum in 1924.

Playing at home and with great discipline, St. Charles held a rangier, heavily favored Batavia team (18–2) to a 3-point Little Seven victory on February 6, 1959. Ho-hum? The final score was 3–0!

St. Charles controlled the ball and took five shots, all in the closing seconds of a quarter, but missed all five. Batavia took two, one in the first 15 seconds that produced a 2–0 lead and one on the game's final play. St. Charles coach George Baptist, recalling that his boys had lost, 49–33, just two weeks before when they had tried to run with Batavia, reasoned that a legal stall was his only possible solution.

St. Charles moved the ball enough to stay within the rules. The 1,200 spectators were transfixed. Most of them empathized with Baptist and/or saw clinical drama in the cat-and-mouse proceedings. Could the home team just maybe win this way? Could an upset come at the buzzer?

If this were the Westville district tournament on March 6, 1930, when Georgetown nipped Homer, 1–0, the teams would have occasionally sat on the floor while the officials took seats in the stands. If it were nearby Catlin on February 4, 1930, when Rossville defeated the hosts, 5–0, in overtime, there would have been open hostility in the crowd. The Catlin principal unplugged the gymnasium clock when he noticed the Rossville players staring at it.

If this were the district tournament at Rocky Ford, Colorado, on March 7, 1941, when La Junta and Las Animas were 0–0 at the end of regulation time, there would have been booing and bitterness in the stands, with one of the bands playing a funeral dirge. One newspaper, calling the winning basket "lucky," asked why teams practiced all year for a performance like this.

Not so in St. Charles, Illinois, in 1959. The home crowd more or less understood. But, needless to say, both teams were well rested for their next encounters—on the following night.

Nineteen fifty-two was not a very good year. It was the "Year of the Free Throw," paved with good intentions that almost ruined the game. There was wholesale foul-calling, and from coast to coast fans witnessed endless processions to the free throw stripe. The rules makers had tried to kill two birds with one stone: curb increasing rough play as well as the increasing number of fouls being called. As antidotes they allowed a "two-to-make-one" before the final three minutes; that is, a player received a second free throw only if he *missed* the first. During the final three minutes every foul incurred two throws.

The legislation was a failure. With free throwing suddenly the main attraction, fans were certain this was not what basketball was meant to be. At Elgin on November 29, 1952, the host team and opponent Proviso were whistled 77 times, and 120 free throws were attempted. Elgin converted 46 of 64, Proviso 33 of 56. A foul was called every 25 seconds.

It took two years to change the rule to a variant of the current one-and-one bonus. Free throwing is still important, but the tail no longer wags the dog.

"It's our Picasso, our Sears Tower," an ex-Chicagoan turned Quincy radio broadcaster says of high school basketball's lofty position in his adopted community. When he says "basketball is our biggest source of pride," he reflects a general sentiment in hundreds of communities across America's heartland. High school ball is an activity in which the small town, without universities or great cultural outlets, can be competitive.

Not all good ideas survive in the competitive world. Junior basketball— for boys five-eight or five-seven and under at various times—flourished in the Chicago Public League from 1936 to 1952. It lasted a few years longer in the city's Catholic League. Before the junior era there was lightweight basketball, and each category produced exciting teams considered, rightly or wrongly, the equal of the better senior or heavyweight contenders.

The most storied Chicago junior players of all time were the Marshall Commandos, who amassed 98 consecutive victories from December 1939 to March 1944, won four city titles in the process, and were at least half the drawing card for the national record crowd of 21,472 that jammed the Chicago Stadium on March 28, 1943, for the all-city championship finals. Sporting an 80-game streak at that juncture, Marshall defeated Mount Carmel by a glorified baseball score, 21–12. Mount Carmel's seniors routed Kelvyn Park, coming off a close defeat by Paris's state champions in the quarterfinals at Champaign, 48–24.

Possessing great speed and deft ball-handling, the Commandos had stirred the national media as early as the 1941–42 season. Izzy Acker, who went on to the University of Michigan, was the star then. A national magazine did a pictorial feature on the Commandos, a caption asking, "Is This America's Greatest High School Basketball Team?" Readers were never quite certain whether the editors thought an outstanding five-eight team could handle an outstanding any-height opponent or whether they didn't know this *was* a five-eight team.

The veteran 1942–43 team consisted of Morrie Kaplan, Hyman "Pee Wee" Tadelman, Chickie Zomlefer, Irving Maser, and Dave Levitan. It was probably the best of the lot. The 1943–44 team was clearly down a bit, but it added 17 more victories to the string before a 40–35 loss to Parker in the Public League semifinals at St. Sabina Community Center finally burst the bubble.

Picturesque team nicknames in Illinois include several with historical, economic, or environmental connotation.

Among the historical are the Lincoln Railsplitters, La Salle-Peru Cavaliers, St. Patrick Shamrocks, Farragut Admirals, Bunker Hill Minutemen, Lexington Minutemen, Wellington Dukes, Egyptian (Tamms) Pharaohs, Shabbona Indians, and Polo Marcos.

Among the economic and environmental are the Kewanee Boilermakers, Hoopeston-East Lynn Cornjerkers, Joliet Steelmen, Alden-Hebron Green Giants, Coal City Coalers, Gillespie Miners, East Alton-Wood River Oilers, Springfield Senators, Havana Ducks, Henry Mallards, and Freeport Pretzels.

Other inventive Illinois nicknames include the Effingham Flaming Hearts, Teutopolis Wooden Shoes, Mount Carmel (Chicago) Caravan, Chillicothe Grey Ghosts, Weber Red Horde, Monmouth Zippers, Goreville Black Cats, Maria Mystics, and Antioch Sequoits.

While a player's 19th birthday has long been the eligibility cutoff date in Illinois, IHSA rules now mercifully permit athletes reaching that milestone to remain eligible through the season in progress. There were some storied birthday scenarios in former days. In 1960 Willard "Bumpy" Nixon led Galesburg to a sectional championship on Tuesday, celebrated his 19th birthday on Thursday, and was forced to be a spectator at his team's "Sweet 16" opener on Friday. In 1943 Elmo Hilderbrand of Clay City, the state's leading scorer, became "overage" just before the start of regional play. This scenario was shrouded in mystery. Hilderbrand's birth records had been lost, and at an early age he had been given an arbitrary birth date, February 17, 1924. He became ineligible just as the season was reaching its crescendo.

Illinois boys' competition may never yield another career like that of Bruce Douglas, Quincy '82, a four-year regular whose teams' overall record was 123–5. It included a junior-year unbeaten state championship season, a freshman season blemished only by a title-game loss, and a senior season marred only by a "Sweet 16" semifinal defeat. Illinois girls, however, have a worthy contender in Courtney Porter, Hume Shiloh '90, another four-year regular whose teams compiled a 118–6 record in winning four state tournament trophies.

Hebron (now Alden-Hebron) teams became known as "Green Giants" in deference to the extensive neighboring farmland owned by Green Giant Company. As with most corporations, the company's public relations department employed a clipping service to pick up every possible "Green Giant" mention in newspapers and magazines across the nation. The year was 1952, and no one at company headquarters in Minneapolis had instructed the readers to restrict their clipping to corporate references and to disregard items about a sensational small-school basketball team in Illinois. One day a huge package containing thousands of "Green Giant" clippings was delivered to headquarters. Ninety percent of them concerned the team. The clips cost 15 cents apiece. A PR person dashed to the phone to clarify the ground rules.

In 1976, during his sixth term as mayor of Chicago, Richard J. Daley was dedicating a park district field house on the South Side. As dignitaries congregated near one of the baskets, two young aides tried clumsy, unsuccessful shots. Thereupon the 74-year-old Daley took the ball himself, eyed the hoop, bent slightly, and fired a two-hand set shot, the style of his De La Salle high school days just after World War I. He smiled as it swished. Forty-five minutes later he died of a heart attack.

PART II

INDIANA

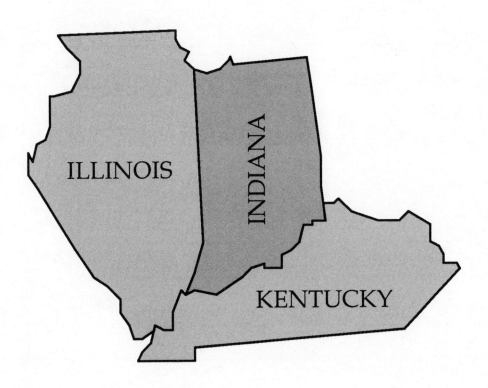

MAGNIFICENT
OBSESSION

---

*In general, young Indiana high school basketball
coaches are about as secure in their jobs and as
immune from alumni pressure as young Division I
college football coaches. When it's a one-school
community and basketball is the only game in town,
winning can become obsessive in the public mind. The
town's image is perceived to be at stake. Monday
morning quarterbacks abound. Only the gods know all
of what prep coaches go through in the effort to achieve
the best possible win-loss records and get their teams
up for the play-offs, but Bruce Newman, writing in a
1985 issue of* Sports Illustrated, *revealed some of it.
In the process he captured much of the Hoosier state's
basketball lore. Following is a major part of that story.*

It was nearly midnight when the patrol car slid slowly through the high
school parking lot, its tires hissing softly on the rain-slicked pavement.
Stopping, the car spat the beam from its spotlight against the wall of the
school. The beam moved methodically back and forth, occasionally form-
ing luminous puddles in the classroom windows, when it suddenly picked
up a solitary figure hustling toward the gym door. There would be questions to answer. Mike Copper put his head down and kept walking.

Copper is the basketball coach at Warren Central High in Indianapolis,
the third-largest school in Indiana. He's 37 but looks young enough that,
in the dark, he can pass for one of his players, which is one reason Copper
had a problem with the officer when he tried to open the gym that night.
Every time he tried to explain that the Indiana basketball season would
officially begin one second past midnight, Monday, October 8, 1984, the
lawman snorted at him.

"But why midnight?" the officer wanted to know.

"We want to get a jump on the rest of the state," Copper replied,
clapping. "We call it Midnight Madness."

With that, the officer snorted and squinted again, as if he were trying to commit Copper's face to memory.

"Bringing a bunch of high school kids out to play basketball at 12 o'clock on a school night," he said, "must be some kind of madness all right."

In the gym, at exactly midnight, Copper threw a basketball into the air, and when it came down, 38 young Hoosiers dived on it as if it were a dream just fallen from the sky. Before the month was out, almost half of them would be cut. "That's the hardest part of the job," Copper said. "You're taking away their dream. I tell the kids, 'You can no longer be a successful basketball player, but that doesn't mean you can no longer be a successful person.' It's hard to make them believe that, though, because in Indiana those two things are so intertwined."

As the players continued to battle each other for possession of the ball, Jerry Watts sat in the bleachers, watching, focusing on his son, Kwame, a 15-year-old sophomore trying out for the Warren Central Warriors. "Kwame means born on a Saturday," said Watts. "It's a Ghanaian name. He was born when African names were in vogue." Watts seemed slightly sheepish about this. A slender man with rimless glasses, he kept saying that for kids to be practicing basketball until 1:30 in the morning was indeed "crazy." But he was obviously enjoying himself and hoping that his son would make the team. If not, Watts knew that in a city the size of Indianapolis, Kwame would have other things to do besides playing basketball. "When I was growing up, that was the only outlet we had," he said, nodding at the floor, "bouncing that ball."

Bouncing the ball was precisely what junior Duane Sharpe was doing at that very moment as he made a beeline for one of the baskets. When his shot, the first score of the night, banked in, everybody in the gym stopped and applauded. The season had begun. Sharpe smiled bashfully. Six weeks later he would quit the team to become a rodeo cowboy. "He may be the first kid in the history of Indiana high school basketball we ever lost to the rodeo," said Copper.

Last year's high school basketball tournament in California—the most populous state in the U.S. and certainly one of the game's hotbeds—was considered one of the most successful ever, drawing nearly 200,000 spectators to the Division I, II, and III play-offs. Indiana, by contrast, has 18 million fewer people than California and one-third the number of high schools, yet last year 1,036,261 people turned out for the Indiana state tournament, which unlike most others isn't divided into divisions according to the schools' sizes. From Bippus to Birdseye, from Holland to Peru, from places where the gym has more seats than the town has people, from all over Indiana, they came streaming off the farms and out of the auto factories, headed for the games. Before the tip-off, these gentle people had in common but a single secret wish for their teams' opponents. "They all want you to die," says Anderson High coach Norm Held, "and they don't care when. It's almost a kind of insanity. You know, like a cult."

That's Hoosier Hysteria—love and death and lunacy, one of America's goofiest tribal rites. "This isn't a game in Indiana, it's a religion," declares Howard Sharpe, who has coached in the state for 45 years. "There was a year once when nobody was buried in Indiana for a week. Big snowstorm paralyzed everything." Sharpe pauses to let this sink in. "And there were 250 high school basketball games played in the state that week. They just put the people on snowplows and brought 'em to the gyms." Sharpe doesn't say whether these were living people or the dear departed, all dressed up with no place to go.

There's no record of any fans dying *because* of a high school basketball game in Indiana, although over the years there have been some fairly close calls. At a tournament in Delphi during the late 1930s, feelings became so heated that every time referee Joe Dienhart made a call against the Oracles, the highly partisan home crowd jeered and rained debris onto the floor. As the evening wore on, the mood became increasingly ugly, until at last, after a call the fans found particularly unsavory, the entire crowd appeared on the verge of storming the floor in pursuit of Dienhart and his fellow official. Suddenly the Delphi High principal stood up in front of the bleachers and signaled for quiet. This was a relief to Dienhart, but his comfort was short-lived. When the gym had finally settled down to a low boil, the principal spoke. "Boys," he said, addressing himself to the angry crowd before him and jerking a thumb toward the referees behind him, "we know they're crooked. I'm with you on that all the way. All I'm asking you to do is wait and let them finish the game. Then we'll get 'em." On that disquieting note, the game proceeded. When it was over, the two officials, one wielding a baseball bat, had to back their way out of the gym.

It may say something about the rough-and-tumble atmosphere that surrounds basketball in Indiana that the first game in the state was played above a Crawfordsville tavern in the spring of 1893. That was also the first game ever played outside the state of Massachusetts, where basketball was invented in 1891 by Dr. James Naismith. In 1925 Naismith himself journeyed to Indiana for the state high school final and, upon his return home, wrote, "The possibilities of basketball as seen there were a revelation to me." By that time the tournament field had increased from 12 teams in 1911 to 674, and basketball had become a statewide obsession. "Quite literally, the state was wild about it," says John Wooden, who as a junior played on Martinsville High's 1927 state championship team. Wooden, of course, went on to win 10 NCAA titles as the coach at UCLA, but he says, "For a high school player, winning the Indiana state championship was far more meaningful than winning the NCAA is today or has ever been." When Muncie knocked off Martinsville in Wooden's senior year, all the Muncie players were rewarded with new Ford roadsters.

Indiana's reputation as the basketball capital of America gradually spread to other parts of the country. "Thirty years ago, Indiana was where basketball was happening," says Jerry Hoover, who spent 16 years as a high school coach there before becoming an assistant at Indiana State. "If you went into the military and said you were from Indiana, they automatically told you to report to the gym. A lot of guys were saved from KP, guard duty, and generally getting their asses shot off because they were from Indiana." Grantland Rice captured most of what America knew about Indiana in the poem "Back in 1925."

> Round my Indiana Homestead,
> As they sang in days gone by,
> Now the basketballs are flying
> And they almost hide the sky;
> For each gym is full of players
> And each town is full of gyms
> As a hundred thousand snipers
> Shoot their goals with deadly glims.

People in Indiana wouldn't actually say "glims," of course, because they are too practical to use words 'her Hoosiers wouldn't understand— and too stubborn to look up words they know they're never going to hear again. In fact, Hoosiers don't readily accept the unfamiliar, linguistic or otherwise. Probably the best expression of their conservative, eyes-on-the-road philosophy was uttered by a Hoosier congressman named Earl Landgrebe the day before Richard Nixon resigned from office. "Don't confuse me with the facts," said Landgrebe, a staunch Republican. "I've got a closed mind."

Nowhere is that kind of obstinacy more prevalent than in Indiana's small towns, where basketball—with its long tradition and ancient rivalries—is the strongest thread running through the most close-knit communities. "In the little towns, people sometimes run for the school board on a platform of nothing more than wanting to fire the basketball coach," says Hoover. "In Indiana, everybody thinks he's a coach because he either played basketball or studied the game. And usually he knows what the hell he's talking about."

When Copper went to Paoli in 1969 to interview for his first head coaching job, he was surprised to discover that the school board exercised control over the hiring and firing of only two school employees, the high school principal and the basketball coach. "During the interview, a board member actually jumped up and asked me to show him my end out-of-bounds play," says Copper. He wound up taking the job and spending three years in Paoli, a town of about 3,300 people, with a gym that seats 4,433. This is in Orange County, one of the poorest in the state.

The size of that gym probably said a good deal about priorities in Paoli. The basketball rivalry between Paoli High and the Stonecutters of neighboring Bedford High had become so bitter during the 1960s that the Paoli school board decided to make a direct and brutal assault on the Stonecutters' prestige. At that time Bedford had the biggest gym in the area, which generally meant that every season it hosted its own 10-team sectional—the first round of the state tournament played at 64 sites, followed by the 16 regionals, 4 semi-states, and final 4. At the urging of one of its members, the Paoli board poured all of its building funds into the construction of a gym that seated 400 more spectators than Bedford's. The following year Paoli, whose gym was now the showpiece of the county, became host to a sectional of its own.

When Copper arrived in Paoli, he found a world where daily life orbited almost completely around the two biggest buildings in town—the gym and the church. "They weren't going to the opera in Paoli," he says. "In southern Indiana, church and basketball are the focal points of people's lives, and as the basketball coach, your status is probably about as high as the local preacher's. If you live in Paoli, there are no other activities, unless you count driving over to Louisville to look at the moving staircases. If those people aren't going to the basketball game on Friday night, they're not doing anything."

Even in failing health, Sharpe, 69, hasn't been able to let go of Friday nights. Last June he underwent a heart catheterization, at which time his surgeon discovered that one of the arteries that had been used in a double-bypass operation in 1982 had become 100 percent blocked. But Sharpe, who's the second-winningest coach in the history of the state, needs just 20 victories at North Knox High to surpass the 734 chalked up by Marion Crawley from 1931–67 at Greencastle, Washington, and Lafayette Jefferson. Sharpe is going to prove himself an immortal or die trying. "He's in a profession that's pretty tough on a younger man," says Tom Oliphant, 38, a rival coach at tiny L & M High, "and he's had some problems with his heart. But if he won the game that gave him the record for most wins, then keeled over on the floor, I believe he'd die a happy man."

Two days after Thanksgiving, most of the corn in Greene County is already down. The day has been balmy, and now as the light slips lower and lower in the sky, a thin layer of blue wood smoke settles over the rolling stubble fields. At the L & M High School gym just south of Lyons, people are already taking their seats for tonight's game with Eastern High of Bloomfield. Because space in the 1,275-seat gym is first come, first served, L & M fans have been lined up in a corridor outside the gym since 5:00 P.M. The varsity game won't begin until 8:20 and won't end before 10:00. "It just became the thing to do last year," says Clyde Earl Hostetter. "It got so these people would show up at a quarter of six even for games where they knew there'd be plenty of room. It kind of intimidated them other teams to walk in from their buses and find a gym already full of people, I guess. Now everybody just keeps coming earlier and earlier."

Clyde Earl and his brothers, K.D. and Elmer, farm 2,300 acres of beans and corn around Lyons and Marco, the two towns whose schools consolidated 27 years ago to form L & M. Today the school has 132 students. Early in the basketball season, when game days come during the harvest, the Hostetter brothers do double duty so they can be sure to get to the gym in plenty of time.

L & M fans have been waiting for this season to get going for a long time. "This man who was about 70 years old came up to me one day," says Oliphant. "He looked me right in the eye and said, 'I don't have much time left on this earth, but I wish some of the time I do have would hurry up and go by so the basketball season would get started.' "

L & M could be this year's miracle team, and nobody would want to miss being part of that. The tiny school isn't supposed to be able to compete with the powers from the north, like Marion and Muncie Central. Yet last season the Braves were 23–0 before losing to Terre Haute South in the Terre Haute regional. As of last week, L & M, led by three seniors, 6'6½" Jeff Oliphant, the coach's son, 6'5½" Tony Patterson, and 6'4" Chad Grounds, were 18–1 and ranked Number 4 in the state. In fact, the Braves were Number 1 in the UPI coaches' preseason poll. A 61–59 loss in December to the top-rated team, South Bend Adams, caused L & M to drop to Number 5. Adams was the first team L & M played this year with any black players on its roster, not to mention the first team the Braves had faced whose starting guards and center had shaved their uniform numbers into their scalps.

During basketball season, each week in Lyons is an agony of waiting that begins in church on Sunday, after which most of the men head over to Mike's garage. This isn't the kind of small-town filling station where everybody goes to watch a car get its tires rotated. It's just a garage, with a potbellied stove and a barber chair instead of a car in it, out back of Mike Terrell's house. Terrell is a 37-year-old biology teacher at L & M. It is a place where the men sit and talk about ball. Hoosiers rarely refer to the game by any other name but "ball." "Mike's pretty proud of his garage," Tom Oliphant says.

Oliphant is a 1964 graduate of L & M, and after a lackluster college baseball career at Indiana State, he followed in the footsteps of his father, who had coached basketball for 18 years, though never at L & M. "I moved away for 17 years, got married, and then came back," is the way Oliphant describes his odyssey. The distant shores he came back from were Linton and Worthington—12 and 13 miles, respectively, from Lyons. "When we left Worthington," says Oliphant's wife, Renee, "there was a lot of dissension because people felt we were deserting them. There were a lot of rumors that Tom was taking a cut in pay because L & M had such a good team. That was crazy, of course, but you know, people get their feelings involved."

In most Indiana towns there are small groups of men who meet almost every morning and, over coffee, second-guess the local coach. In Lyons, the fraternity of drugstore coaches meets at Hamilton Pharmacy, and the Hostetter brothers are senior members. In fact, K.D. holds the rather august title of Drugstore Athletic Director—or, simply, K.D. the A.D. The drugstore coaches proved their clout in Lyons two years ago when they got up a petition against Dave Henson, who was then the L & M coach, and got him fired.

During winter, petitions fly like snowflakes in Indiana. The community that hasn't used one to get rid of a coach is rare indeed. The owner of a gas station in one northern Indiana town decided he wanted to get the local high school coach fired, so he had every customer who drove into his station sign his petition. He even got people with out-of-state license plates to sign. Everything was rolling along smoothly until a woman who drove in for a fill-up turned out to be the coach's wife.

Actually, there were two petitions circulated around the drugstore in Lyons two years ago. One was to get rid of Henson, and the second was a sort of grass-roots nomination drive for Oliphant. "We knew Tom because he's from here," says K.D. the A.D. "We knew he was a good coach. And, of course, we knew he had Jeff."

Henson's shortcomings, whatever they may have been, didn't include excessive losing. L & M was 14–7 the year he was fired. Henson, it seems, never tried to be popular with the people. The drugstore coaches form the Hoosier equivalent of a Greek chorus on this subject.

"He wasn't active in the community," says K.D.

"He was hard to talk to," says Gordon Grounds, Chad's father.

"I think," says Bob Montgomery, summing up, "his problem was he lived in Linton."

In this evening's game, the Eastern High Thunderbirds' main problem with L & M is anatomical, not geographical: Eastern's biggest player is 6'2". From there the drop is rather precipitous, down to one starter who measures 5'4½".

Just a few minutes before the tip-off, the gym gets an almost palpable jolt when Indiana University coach Bob Knight and an assistant arrive to scout Jeff Oliphant. This is an event occasioning such intense communal pride that as the news of Knight's presence travels around the gym, heads turn and necks are craned. Knight merely stands in one corner of the arena, desultorily eating popcorn.

L & M leads 24–12 at the end of the first quarter and then runs off 22 straight points to go ahead 46–12. In the midst of all this there's a better drama going on. On the bench, the elder Oliphant has spotted Knight, still eating popcorn, and as the game progresses his eyes frequently wander back to the corner where Knight is standing. When Patterson, L & M's leading scorer and a candidate for the state's coveted title of Mr. Basketball, takes a long shot that rattles off the rim, Oliphant the coach barks "pass off once in a while" and then looks anxiously at Knight again.

Knight and his aide abruptly turn and march out of the gym with three minutes left in the first half. When Oliphant discovers that the object of all his attention has disappeared from sight, he begins to edge farther and farther down the sideline, trying to get a better angle on the corner where Knight had been standing. Soon he's almost oblivious to the game, intently following the popcorn trail with his eyes, until finally he finds himself practically in the lap of Gary Cook, the Thunderbirds' startled coach. When it becomes clear that Knight has vanished, Oliphant turns back toward his bench, still preoccupied with Knight's sudden departure. (Jeff plans to enroll at Indiana in the fall and try to make Knight's team, as a walk-on.)

After the game, which the Braves won 98–47, L & M's boosters are invited out to the home of assistant coach Larry Hasler. Hasler raises about 100 hogs on his farm, but most of the talk at the party is about basketball futures. The coaches and their wives get into a discussion about the bloodlines of prospective L & M players, hoping to determine which of the local progeny are likely to grow big enough to post up the coal miner's sons from Shakamak. "His father's six-foot," Oliphant will say ruminatively, "but he had an uncle on his mother's side who was real big." This is followed by a long, thoughtful pause. "And his grandmother was tall."

Outside, under a waxing moon, the hogs grow fatter and fatter. Soon it will be time for them to go to market.

Four little-known facts about Indiana: (1) In 1950, the state had more hogs than it had people; (2) the restaurant in Bloomington, where Hoagy Carmichael wrote "Star Dust" and "Georgia on My Mind," is now a pizza-by-the-slice parlor; (3) Halston, the chic New York fashion designer, is from Evansville, Indiana, a fact he rarely brings up at parties [editor's note: Halston died in March 1990]; (4) In 1974, Indiana's Mr. Basketball—a title that has been won by such Hoosier legends as Robertson, Rick Mount, and George McGinnis—was shared by Steve Collier of Southwestern and Roy Taylor of Anderson. Fourth in the balloting that year was a skinny senior from French Lick, name of Larry Bird.

There was probably never a Mr. Basketball who lived the title as obsessively as Steve Alford of New Castle. In 1965, when Steve was a year old and just beginning to dribble, his parents, Sam and Sharan Alford, sent out Christmas cards inscribed with the prediction that he would one day be Mr. Basketball. In 1983 he was. Alford started playing ball when he was four and was soon spending so much time in gyms with his father, the New Castle Chrysler High coach, that he learned to count by reading scoreboards and learned to read by sounding out the names on the backs of players' uniforms. "I don't know if the right word to describe Steve would be unique, unusual, or just odd," says Sam. "He was always obsessed with basketball. There would be nights at 11:00 when I'd hear that ball bouncing out in the driveway and know that Steve couldn't sleep."

"When Steve went in to see the junior high counselors and they asked him what his long-range career goals were," says Sharan, "he put down that he was going to be a professional basketball player. When they told him he had to put down something else, Steve couldn't believe it. Here he was, this scrawny little eighth grader, but he *knew*. He came home that day very upset with his counselor, almost with tears in his eyes. 'Mom,' he said, 'she doesn't believe I can make it.' "

Alford hasn't made it yet, but he's right on schedule. He shot 60 percent from the field and 94.4 percent from the foul line and averaged 37.2 points a game as a senior at New Castle. Then as a freshman last year at Indiana University he led the Hoosiers to the NCAA East Regional final. Last summer he was the youngest player on the gold medal-winning U.S. Olympic team. As an Olympian he played in an exhibition game before 67,596 people in—where else?—the Hoosier Dome. It was the largest crowd ever to attend a basketball game. During his four years at New Castle, Alford played his home games in the largest high school gymnasium, capacity 9,325, in the world.

In fact, the smallest gym in the North Central Conference, of which New Castle is one of eight members, in Logansport, holds 5,830 people. New Castle's gym holds a few more fans than the 8,996 that regularly squeeze into Anderson High's Wigwam, but in the Wigwam they take their basketball so seriously that the crowds seem even larger. The Indians have been to the state championship game three times in the last six seasons, losing by four, then two, and finally by one excruciating point in 1983 to Connersville. "Each time it takes people weeks to get over it," says Belinda Kinder, an Anderson superfan. "Some people have to go to the doctor. It's like a death."

There are actually three high schools in Anderson (population 65,000)—Highland, Madison Heights, and Anderson—and taken together, they attract almost 12,000 season-ticket holders shelling out an average of $15 for 11 games. In 1980, the city of Anderson had the highest unemployment rate in the nation at 22½ percent. "It's such a strong rivalry here that it's really like three different cities," says Brenda Weinzapfel, treasurer of the Indians' booster club. "We hate Highland, and they hate us so much that after a while it affects your thinking." For instance, Weinzapfel refuses to shop in the Highland district. "No Indian fan would go out to Highland to buy something if they could buy it in a store owned by another Indian," she says.

Belinda and her husband, Terry Kinder, have missed only one Anderson High road game in four years, and they haven't missed a home game in eight years, despite the fact that from 1980–83 Terry was laid off for a total of 20 months from the local GM plant where he works. The Kinders recently moved from a single-wide trailer home to a double-wide so Terry would have more room for the $1,500 worth of Indian statuary and memorabilia he has collected. Belinda does her part by working as a baker in the school cafeteria, which entitles her to basketball tickets when Anderson plays in the tournament. "We don't have any fringe benefits, no insurance or anything," she says, "but a couple of years ago they started making sure that all the school employees would be able to buy two tickets to every Indians tournament game. They couldn't have given me anything better than that." Somewhere out there in his grave, another old Hoosier, socialist labor organizer Eugene V. Debs, must be spinning like a lathe.

There are 29 families in Anderson who have held season tickets to the Indians' games for 50 years or more. And Louise Greve, whose husband, Arnold, bought a pair of season tickets a year before America heard its first licensed radio broadcast, has been going to games for 64 years. At 83, Greve still jumps to her feet when she disagrees with a referee's call and frequently holds out her glasses to the offending zebra. "You can't see, Buster," she bellows. "Do you want these?"

Times are good for the 13–5 Indians now, and Louise Greve rarely misses a game. She has told the school's athletic director that when her time comes, she wants her 40-year-old grandson, Steve Hedgecraft, to have her tickets. "But he don't get 'em till I'm gone," she says. Then she turns her gaze back to the basketball court, where young boys who probably couldn't conceive of a world without MTV, much less radio or slam dunks, are shooting lay-ups and clapping hands.

"Arnold would always say, it don't matter if they have a good team or not, we're gonna support 'em," she says. "We were just *fans*, that's all."

THE STEREOTYPE

*If you were a casting director back in the sixties, in
search of the quintessential Hoosier basketball player,
you'd likely have turned immediately to Rick Mount,
Lebanon High '66 and Purdue '70. He fit the stereotype
completely. An unassuming small-town boy who made
it big. A great pure shooter who broke state and Big 10
scoring records, averaging 27.3 points in high school
and 32.3 in college. The son of a father who had been
a star in the same hometown. A four-year high school
regular who had never been far from home and would
play college ball in Indiana. And the first high
school player ever to grace a* Sports Illustrated *cover.
The following Rick Mount article, written by the noted
Frank Deford in 1966, Mount's senior prep year,
appeared in the magazine's cover issue. Its focus is on
an individual, but it mirrors life in a typical
basketball-oriented Hoosier community.*

*Ain't God good to Indiana?
Folks, a feller never knows
Just how close he is to Eden
Till, sometimes, he ups and goes
Seekin' fairer, greener pastures
Than he has right here at home,
Where there's sunshine in the clover
An' there's honey on the comb,
Where th' ripples on the river
Kind of chuckle as they flow—
Ain't God good to Indiana?
Ain't he, fellers? Ain't he though?*

—WILLIAM H. HASKELL
(1873–1930)

Despite such idyllic sentiments, with which all Hoosiers would agree, it soon will be time for Rick Mount to leave Lebanon, Indiana (population 9,523), and attack the bigger world with a basketball. He is eager for the challenge for, though Rick Mount is a small-town Hoosier, he is not Penrod. But the Penrods are gone, just like the small towns all turned pseudosuburban. Penrod was not 6 feet 4 and 179 pounds, neither was he given to alpaca sweaters and tight ankle-high white Levi's, nor to wing-tip shoes that you get at the "Red" Apple Shoe Store. And he did not have a tricky man-made curl hanging over his forehead, a curl that only Dobby or Gerald down at the Modern Barber Shop is capable of cutting properly.

Rick Mount does fish for crappies and channel cat out in Cool Lake, and he wanders through the woods outside of town hunting for rabbits with his beagle Bootsy at his side, but he also has a lavender '57 Chevy convertible and a pretty little blonde who wants to be a dental technician, and he takes her to the Sky Vue Drive-In and to the Tom Boy for Cokes and 19-cent hamburgers. He works extra hard to get Bs and Cs in Spanish, biblical literature, English, and government in a sparkling, modern high school that is fashioned in the popular hues of Holiday Inn green and Howard Johnson orange. It is now complete with windows ripped full of buckshot holes by juvenile delinquents that they have not caught yet — exactly like in the big city.

So sunshiny clover and chuckling ripples notwithstanding, Indiana is going to have a tall time holding onto Rick Mount, who may be as good a high school basketball player as there ever was. He has the moves of a cat, Mr. Haskell; the eyes of a hawk, the presence of a king, and he has visions of UCLA or Cincinnati or Miami or other faraway places. Coaches come clamoring to him. Not just the recruiters, but men like Vic Bubas of Number 1 Duke and old Adolph Rupp of Number 2 Kentucky and John Wooden of champion UCLA and Bruce Hale of Miami, who was so solicitous as to phone Rick last spring when he heard that a tornado had cut by just north of Lebanon. And, like gunslingers, the kids come from all over the state — the white farm boys and the Negroes from downtown Indianapolis — just for the chance to challenge him on the outdoor summer court in the Lebanon park.

Comparisons are obligatory because Oscar Robertson played in high school just 26 miles away, down what is now Interstate, in Indianapolis, and many people have seen them both. When Rick was just a sophomore, Ray Crowe, Oscar's coach at Crispus Attucks High, said: "At this stage he's as good as Oscar was." Most fans, like Pistol Sheets, who runs the town pool hall, agree with this analysis. Pistol expresses the consensus this way: "Rick is a better shooter than anyone you ever saw in high school, but Arsker" — that's the way they pronounce Oscar in Lebanon, Indiana — "now Arsker, he had the better maneuverability."

Rick is modest, as heroes, particularly small-town ones, are supposed to be. His emotions are controlled, particularly on the court, where he seldom expresses himself with more than an occasional single loud hand clap. Despite his blond hair and blue eyes, his high cheekbones create a decided Indian effect. He is shocked when anyone compares him with his idol, Robertson, even with the Big O's high school phase. Rick is, in fact, unspoiled by notoriety, except in a negative way, freezing with embarrassment when strange grown-ups make a fuss over him in front of his old friends and teammates—Larry Clark and Keith Campbell, whom he drives home from practices; Mike Caldwell and Rick Brown, the little junior guards; Ron Templin, who has some college offers himself; Jeff Tribbett and the others whom he has grown up with. At times, when trapped by a coach under circumstances that he considers confining, he tenses and will not speak at all but will merely nod yes or no—not impolitely, but merely because he is desperate to end such a confrontation.

However, having been witness to Rick's talent for so long, the other players—far from exhibiting the least bit of jealousy that Coach Jim Rosenstihl fears—are not affected one way or another by all the attention paid Mount. They have never played on the Lebanon Tigers without him, so the fuss is status quo for them. Just as serene is Donna Cadger, the very pretty blonde with whom Rick has been going officially since two weeks before Christmas. She has his sweetheart ring, two gold hearts intertwined with a "teensy-weensy" diamond. "Gee," Donna says, "I know it's just Rick. I mean, I've known him all my life. Anyway, you know, I used to go out with him before, back in grade school. The people who get so excited about him are just the grown-ups, like my father. He's just a real nut about basketball." Richard Cadger, as a matter of fact, did nickname Rick "Rocket," and that is what Rick's friends now call him.

Teen-age fame, then, is hardly uncommon in Indiana, but it is the adults and not the crazy kids who are responsible for it. When Rick was playing in the fifth grade, crowds of a thousand or more would show up to watch him. Grown people, grandfathers and grandmothers. They travel 80 or 100 miles one way to see a game that does not even involve their own team. A bunch from Lebanon went that far to see a game in Cloverdale the other night and ran into Tink Bennett from Rossville, and he had come 35 miles farther. Herbie West flagged down a train once to get from Lebanon to a game in Shelbyville. He hitched a ride back with Ham Foster and Claude Wilson, and Ham says Herbie complained all the way home that the officiating had robbed the Tigers of victory, though Lebanon had lost by 45 points. These people go to fifth-grade games, scouting the future for Rosenstihl. They cut work early to attend varsity practice, and since Rosenstihl prohibits talking, they sit huddled together in the southeast corner of the gym, silently attentive as if they were in some holy place. They get together to watch old game movies that they know by heart. Waiting lists for season tickets are impossibly long. Mayor and Mrs. Herb Ransdell have had the same seats at the Lebanon gym (capacity: 2,200) since it was opened in 1931. Last year, for the price of two tickets to the sectionals (the opening round of the state tournament), Dick Perkins and Bob Staton were able to borrow a brand-new $6,000 tractor so that they could get through a blizzard to rescue Daryl Kern at his farm. Daryl is a substitute.

It is in this atmosphere that Rick Mount grew up, but he still does not understand how important he is to Lebanon. His fans, to him, are just neighbors. "Why, you take a guy like Gene Thomas," Rick said, driving into the courthouse square past the Avon Theatre, "he's as good a mechanic as there is in town, I guess, and I'll take my car in to get it fixed, and Gene'll say: 'Hey, keep my car till I get this fixed.' I mean, just like that. His car. Yeah, this town's been good to me. It's my home."

Aside from Rick himself, there is nothing in Lebanon to distinguish it from any other small Midwest town except that its courthouse is supposed to be the only public building in the world that is bisected by a meridian. (No one seems to have the faintest idea *what* meridian.) The town advertises itself as "The Friendly City," and Pistol Sheets says that is right as rain. "Any old stranger comes to town, just wandering through," he says, "and they take him right in and given him something to eat and all he can drink—just about everything maybe but a ticket to the game. Oh, it's friendly all right. There's a lot of card playing in this town. A man loses too much, everyone gets him paid off, and then we bar him from any more games. We take care of our own."

Lebanon, the seat of Boone County, was settled in 1832 by Abner H. Longley. An early account carefully notes: "Longley was the first postmaster, and carried the mail in his hat, consequently the office was not always in the same place." As early as 1843, the direct forerunner of Lebanon High, the county seminary, was holding classes. By the '80s something of an athletic program was in effect, the school had assumed its present name and had moved to the third floor of the "Martin Hohl Building." On the first floor was a saloon, on the second floor were Martin Hohl and family. The principal was a tough West Pointer named Strange N. Cragum, who was renowned for possessing "excellent knowledge of the general behavior of both boys and girls." His way of handling the boys was to make them put on boxing gloves and then beat the tar out of them. Lebanon's first basketball team was fielded in 1907, just 16 years after the sport was invented. In 1911, the first year of the Indiana tournament—a festival that now enlists virtually every school in the state, grosses well over $1 million, and draws more than 1.5 million spectators—Lebanon lost in the finals to neighboring Crawfordsville, 24–17. The next year Lebanon won. One of the six members of that 1912 team was John Porter, who delivered Richard Carl Mount, the only child of Mary Catherine and Paul W. (Pete) Mount, on January 5, 1947. Four years before, Pete, a skinny 6-foot-3 center, had led Lebanon to the state championship game for the first time since the Tigers won in 1918. His records were not broken until Rick took care of them, and Pete played one year of pro ball with the

Sheboygan Redskins of the early NBA. "Old John Mount—that's Pete's father—what a shame he didn't live to see Rick play ball," Claude Wilson said one night recently, just talking high school basketball. "Every year, John would say not to get excited; Pete had the last team to get to the finals and there wouldn't be another one till Rick came along."

"Around our house," Mrs. Mount remembers, "no one ever tripped over little cars or toys—just balls and bats." Rick was obviously a natural athlete, and when he took to eating and then writing left-handed, Pete Mount says he thought for sure he had a southpaw pitcher. But for some reason, Rick has always thrown and shot a ball right-handed. For all practical and basketball purposes, he is ambidextrous. A prolonged strep throat and ear infection forced him to repeat the second grade, and four years ago his parents were divorced, but otherwise Rick's life in Lebanon has hardly been touched by incident. Once, he remembers, he and Ron Edwards got caught shooting pigeons just inside the city limits. His descriptions of the daily routine in Lebanon closely resemble the reminiscences of a boy who was a pretty good guard over on the Fairmount High teams about 17 years ago—James Dean, the late movie actor. There were long walks, mile and mile up the Pennsylvania Railroad tracks with "a huntin' buddy," Alan Adams; time spent hanging around Preston Cain's gun shop or at the Model Sports shop; and the early, solitary hours that Rick still spends fishing with his dog—"and you bring your gun along, because every now and then you might get a shot at a turtle." Later, girls and drive-ins replaced walking down the railroad tracks with Alan Adams, and that is about it, growing up in Lebanon. That and school. And basketball.

Rick excelled in every sport he tried but by his freshman year he had decided to concentrate on basketball; it was about then that he began to sense his potential. "Still," Mrs. Mount says, "I don't think he appreciates yet how very good he really is. I guess he's too wrapped up in it. He keeps a lot to himself anyway. He goes out there all by himself, just fishing and thinking, I guess, and he never lets on if something is bothering him. He'll finally tell me about it about a week or so later, and usually then it isn't a problem anymore. Since it's been just me living with Rick, with no man in the house, I've tried to let him be more independent. I knew that I couldn't make him any more mature myself, so I just gave him a better chance to do it himself."

Rick's dedication to what he considers important led him to pass up a five-day fishing trip to Canada last June because he felt that would be too much time away from basketball. He has been out of Indiana only four times in his life—three times to see basketball games in Louisville and once to play in one in Chicago. He not only practices incessantly, but he possesses the self-discipline to work on the more tedious facets of the game, not just shooting. He was talking along about this one day recently, when all of a sudden he paused and said: "Well, I found this out: if you don't want to do it, that's the time to do it." That would suffice as Rick Mount's credo.

Rosenstihl, considered one of the best young coaches in the state, came from Bluffton to take the Lebanon job in Rick's freshman year. He had heard about the Mount kid, and by the season's opener Rick was a starter. In that first game, as a freshman, Rick took 16 shots, made 5 of them and 12 points against Brownsburg. He went 11 for 17 against Crawfordsville next, averaged 20.4 for the year, and has never scored less than 11 points in a game. High school statistics are notoriously misleading, but Mount's consistency through the difficult schedules that Rosenstihl draws up has left no doubts about his authenticity. (Rosenstihl even had New York's Power Memorial, with Lew Alcindor, lined up for a game last year until a technicality forced cancellation.) Rick averaged 23.6 as a sophomore, 33.1 last year, and has 33.2 so far this season. He is discriminating with his shots but will bomb from 30 feet regularly if he is open. And he hits better than 50 percent, more than 80 percent of his free throws. He passes and dribbles beautifully. Primarily a guard, he often moves into the forecourt or even the pivot. When he has to be, he is a fine rebounder.

But it is his distance shooting that is so fantastic. It is not exaggerating to say that, with the exception of the pros' Jerry West, there is no one in all of basketball who has the quickness and accuracy at long range that Rick Mount has. Right now, it is difficult to assess his defensive ability, but he is so easy an athlete that defense should be no problem once he can concentrate on it under game conditions. He is so valuable to Lebanon that, like many high school superstars, he must neglect defense to avoid being lost on fouls. But he asks no special favors. "Oh, sure," he says, "some of them smart off at me: 'Come on, great Rick,' and stuff like that, but I've got enough to worry about without carrying on conversations out there."

Since Rick was first-string all-Indiana as a sophomore, legions of coaches, self-appointed recruiters, newspapermen, and adoring fans have been dogging him in earnest. Rosenstihl manages to protect him—without cutting his tongue out, the way they did with Alcindor—but the pressure continues to swell. Kenneth Dooley, the young principal at Lebanon, estimates that 250 colleges have sought out Rick in one way or another. For years John Wooden, a native Hoosier, has insisted he was unable to make it from UCLA to the Old-timers Banquet in Indianapolis. This particular 1966, however, Wooden decided to accept the kind invitation. No, he said, he would not be visiting out in Lebanon, but no one thought to inquire if Rick Mount might drop over to the Indianapolis airport. It was a very interesting little tête-à-tête, though the subject matter was apparently somewhat restricted. "Mostly," Rick says, "Mr. Wooden talked about collapsing zones. How everyone would have to collapse on Alcindor."

Rick not only looks the part for southern California, but he has UCLA glittering in his baby blues. He went to a party the other night and they all played a Ouija-board type of game with a card table. Rick smiles somewhat sheepishly when he says the card table indicated he would go to UCLA. This suggests that either Rick sort of helped the table to reach that answer or that UCLA, on top of everything else, also has a lock on the spirit world. Still, Rick does appear to be open-minded on the subject. He also favors Cincinnati, Oscar's alma mater, and there is fierce pressure from nearly everybody in the state for either Indiana University or Purdue. Rick also plans to visit some or all of these other schools after this season: Miami, Kentucky, Kansas, Tennessee, West Virginia, Duke, Michigan, and Bradley.

In Lebanon interest in Rick's choice of a college must be shelved for a while, because the Indiana high school tournament begins next week and government, commerce, public health, and other such mundane matters cannot be considered while the Hoosiers watch high school kids play basketball. If Lebanon is not one of the tournament favorites, it has a respectable chance; until the Tigers are eliminated and Rick plays his last game, there can be no real concern about where he will continue his education. All along, anyway, there has been a remarkably positive air about what it will be like in Lebanon when Rick is gone. The people do not lack appreciation of the talent that they will be losing but, no matter how large a hero he has been, they could never permit him to transcend the only game in town. If he did, it would be very bad indeed in Lebanon when he left. So lately there has been much talk about next year's team, about the value of *balance*, of the good shooting junior guards, Caldwell and Brown, and how it could be really quite a team if Daryl Kern's younger brother Larry can develop at center.

But oh! Will they talk of Rick Mount when he *is* gone! What he did was to make Lebanon special, and not many places population 9,523 ever get a shot at being special. They will remember Rick for that, no matter what he accomplishes somewhere else in all his college and professional games. He's been so good to them. He's been so good for Lebanon, Indiana.

THE MIRACLE
OF MILAN

*For years people would drive out of their way to
Milan, like pilgrims to Lourdes, to see if they could
fathom what made this town so different. It was as if
they might discover in the demeanor of the inhabitants,
in the structure of the buildings, or in the aroma of
the air what had made Milan, for a moment in time,
so formidable. The little town's Cinderella victory in
Indiana's 1954 state final became a loose model for the
motion picture* Hoosiers, *and the legacy will never be
lost in Ripley County. This story—by Lee Aitken and
Bill Shaw from a March 1987 issue of* People Weekly—
tells how deep the legacy is, almost two generations later.

Don't go poking around the basketball lore of Milan (pronounced *My*-lan),
Indiana, without a ready supply of handkerchiefs. The calendar may say
it's been 33 years this month since Milan won the state title in a classic
upset that is the basis for the movie *Hoosiers*; but to this day most every
business in town has a picture of "the boys," and no Milanite of a certain
age can talk about that championship season without tears. "It was wonderful, the town was full of happy people," says Millie Nocks, 68, as she
gazes at a photo of the team on the wall of Rosie Arkenberg's restaurant.
Then, between quiet sobs, she says, "God bless those boys."

Hoosiers is not a literal telling of what is known as "the Miracle of
Milan." Screenwriter Angelo Pizzo, who grew up in Bloomington, says
he was inspired by what happened in 1954 but not bound by it. True,
one player's father was an alcoholic, and so is Dennis Hopper's character.
But it's not so that star forward Bobby Plump (called Jimmy Chitwood
in the movie) sat out half the season or that the team had only six players:
There were ten. A few folks are sore that Milan was not one of the Indiana
locations for the film, or even mentioned at all, and even Rosie, an admirer
of the film, quibbles with the scenes showing fans in bib overalls. "We
went to the games in our finest clothes," she says. Just the same, the people
of Milan love *Hoosiers*. A newspaper in Indianapolis asked Bobby Plump

to review it and he took a notebook to the theater, but he cried so much he forgot to write anything down. "Those boys that made the movie are Hoosiers," he says. "They understand us."

Plump is 50 now and runs the Bobby Plump Insurance Agency in Indianapolis, but he is still recognized all over the state as the boy who wrought the Miracle. First, he led Milan to a semifinal victory over all-black Crispus Attucks of Indianapolis, whose star was Oscar Robertson, later of the Milwaukee Bucks. Then came Muncie Central, which was 13 times Milan's student-body size. Near the end, with the score tied, Plump held onto the ball for four heart-stopping minutes, then his last-second jump shot sailed up and swish, the Miracle.

"I don't see how there can be any more thrill in a Hoosier kid's life than what happened to me," says Plump, then a shy kid who suddenly was giving speeches all over the state. Like his teammates—who get together in town every Easter—he readily says the win "changed my life." Nine of the players got college scholarships, an unprecedented number for Milan, which that year enrolled only 73 boys.

"When it happened, we were celebrities," says team member Ray Craft, who married cheerleader Virginia Voss and is now the state's commissioner of high school basketball. "And we still are." Of course Indiana basketball is about winning, and not even Craft was immune when back in Milan as coach, his record slipped to 11–10 in his fourth season and he quit. So he sympathizes with Kelly Simpson, the new coach: He ended his first year at 1–18 and jokes, nervously, "I guess they won't be making a movie about us."

Milan never made it back to the state finals. Marvin Wood, the 1954 coach, who is now a guidance counselor, admits, "Nothing's ever come close to that moment. I peaked when I was 26, and I've enjoyed it for 33 years." Well, so has the town. The years haven't been awfully kind: There is no theater any more, the furniture store burned down, and all seven doctors have left town. But Milan's got great memories.

Lee Aitken and Bill Shaw/*People Weekly* © 1987 Time Inc.

FULL CIRCLE

Some day, perhaps in an afterlife, colleges will force star athletes to meet standard academic requirements and not dump them into a cruel, demanding world once their eligibility has run out. College presidents will reclaim their sovereign authority over athletic departments, coaches will no longer be tempted to recruit illegally, and otherwise intelligent alumni will no longer sell their souls for a few extra baskets and touchdowns. Under-the-table payments, forged transcripts, and the spectacles of grown men begging for the services of barely literate teenagers will be forgotten foibles of the corrupt past. Most of today's exploited college athletes were coddled or "socially promoted" through high school. In these competitive days who has the nerve to declare an all-stater ineligible? Sammy Drummer was the darling of Muncie in 1975. He was maneuvered through several colleges, and if he had made the NBA, which only a tiny percentage of college regulars do, he might have finessed his academic shortcomings. But he didn't, and life got empty fast. The following, by Sam Heys of the Atlanta Journal-Constitution, *was voted one of the best sports stories of 1985 by* The Sporting News.

Sammy Drummer hopes he's never asked to sweep the basketball court. Having to clean the backboards with Windex is embarrassing enough.

"Sometimes before a game we have to go over and wipe down the backboard," he says. "That brings back old memories. I say, 'Why am I up here?' "

Drummer played basketball for three colleges and now is cleaning for one.

Five years ago Drummer was one of Georgia Tech's finest players ever. Now he is 28 and a janitor at Ball State University in his home town of Muncie, Indiana, earning $13,228 a year. He wears a ring of 40 keys on a belt loop and worn-out leather Converse basketball shoes on his feet.

"I sit back now and I think about the way things turned out, and at times tears just pop into my eyes," he says. "It's a funny feeling."

Drummer's story is that of a college athlete who didn't get his degree, didn't make it in the pros as he had dreamed he would, and has little to show for the four years he spent in college except a scrapbook of memories.

"He was used. They just used him until they were done with him," says Drummer's high school coach, Myron Dickerson, of Drummer's college years. "It's ironic that Ball State wanted Sam as bad as anybody and now he's back over there. He's made the circle."

His case is not an isolated one. "The circumstances are typical almost to being a composite of what happens on the average, to black athletes in particular, and to white athletes to some extent," says Dr. Harry Edwards, a professor of sociology at the University of California at Berkeley who testified this summer before a Senate subcommittee investigating the academic integrity of college athletics.

A study by the National Collegiate Athletic Association released this summer revealed that only about half of the athletes who entered major universities on athletic scholarships in 1977 graduated within six years. The study included 6,804 athletes at 206 participating institutions in the NCAA's Division I, which includes the majority of America's largest colleges.

"What this means," says Edwards, "is that these Division I schools are running plantations and the kids are not getting educated. As long as there is an endless supply of 20th century gladiators being created in the black communities of this country by parents who are blindly orienting their children to become athletes, why should these schools be concerned about what happens to any particular black athlete?"

Dr. Doug Conner, executive director of the American Association of Collegiate Registrars and Admissions Officers, believes some athletes have not graduated because they "major in eligibility."

"One of the problems has been that athletes could go to college and could just take courses to keep themselves eligible but not necessarily work toward any kind of degree," he says.

Drummer majored in industrial management at Georgia Tech and needed approximately two more years of academic work to graduate when his athletic eligibility expired in '79.

He was admitted to Tech from DeKalb Community College in '77 despite having no algebra in high school or college and scoring only 500 total on the Scholastic Aptitude Test, with 400 being the minimum and 1600 the maximum.

"He is certainly not typical of the ones (athletes) we get," says Dr. Joseph Pettit, Georgia Tech president. "We've got a different coach now and a different athletic director. I'm not saying we might not take a Sammy Drummer, but we are certainly putting education way out front. Our overall policy is to try to get students who can get through. He was really not a very good prospect academically from the start. I think our standards are somewhat higher now.

"I think a young fellow like that takes his chances. We certainly have to tell him that maybe only 1 percent ever get into the pros. I think that's really terribly unfortunate. A student with those kind of scores comes with a disadvantage."

Drummer was behind in school before he ever started. Growing up along the dirt roads of Bolivar County in the Delta country of northwest Mississippi, Drummer didn't enter school until he was 10. Because of his age, he was placed in the third grade.

After his first school year, his mother moved the family to Muncie. "I didn't want to raise my children in the South like I was raised," says Elizabeth Drummer, who had supported her family by chopping and picking cotton. "I knew if I stayed down there, they'd have to do the same thing. I wasn't about to let them work in no field."

Drummer was placed in the fifth grade in Muncie, perhaps because he was two years older than most fourth-graders. He therefore missed three of the first four grades of school.

Basketball became Drummer's life in Indiana, as he no longer had to be satisfied with shooting a balled-up rag at a five-gallon can as he had in Mississippi.

He could dunk a basketball in the seventh grade, and when he injured his knee in the ninth grade and was placed in a hip-to-ankle cast, he still practiced shooting, even in the snow. He would often play until 3 or 4 A.M. on the court next to the public housing project where he lived with his mother, three sisters, and brother.

In high school Drummer was bused across town to Northside, an upper-middle-class school with a 10 percent black enrollment. In a state where high school basketball is a major event and in a city where rival Central High had won more state championships than any Indiana school, the 6-foot-5 Drummer was possibly Muncie's most famous citizen.

"He was a popular kid. He wasn't a bragger or show-off or trouble-maker or anything like that," says Dickerson, his Northside coach. "He'd do anything to play basketball."

To play basketball, Drummer had to remain academically eligible, and that was a struggle.

"School was hard because I was having so much problem with the little stuff, stuff that I should have learned in earlier grades but didn't even know," he says. "If it wasn't for basketball, I wouldn't have gone as far as I did in school. But basketball kind of gave me a boost and made me try hard.

"I wanted to learn. I really didn't want to be dumb all my life."

When Drummer was in the 11th grade, his English teacher, Barbara Pugh, realized that he didn't know that letters had specific sounds. So she bought a phonics workbook designed for children learning to read and worked with him during her free time. Drummer's reading improved and by the time he was out of her class, he was reading on a fourth-grade level.

Both teachers and students would work with Drummer individually. "You'd have to sit around after class," he says, "and sort of like take class all over again."

"He'd stay after school and a lot of teachers would be willing to help him. I mean really help him," says Sonny Burks, a Muncie policeman who moonlighted as a security officer at Northside and became a friend and adviser to Drummer.

Asked if Drummer was "socially promoted" through high school, Northside principal Owen Lemna replies, "Sam was a young man who was friendly and had a smile on his face. He got along with people, he was courteous, he was pleasant. You can draw your own conclusions from that."

Needing a 2.0 grade average to receive an NCAA scholarship, Drummer graduated from Northside in 1957 with a 2.13 average of a possible 4.0. He had not received a college-preparatory education, however.

Six of Drummer's 37½ credits were in industrial arts and eight were split among art, typing, physical education, health, and driver education. His science was limited to physical science, he had no foreign language, and his seven semesters of English were spent in "reading lab," an individualized program for students unable to read at grade level.

Drummer scored only 210 on the verbal half of the SAT college board and 290 on the math half, with 200 being the minimum on each half. But because of his basketball ability, he received scholarship offers from 300 or 400 colleges. He was ranked among the top five high school basketball players in the U.S.

His recruitment became an ordeal he wanted to run away from, often hiding upstairs when recruiters came to his door. "It was a mess, I mean a mess," says Drummer. "I didn't have no one to sit down and tell me what it was all about. All I knew is I had all these coaches coming in from all directions."

Drummer signed a Big Ten letter-of-intent with Indiana but later changed his mind. "I don't think I could have played ball there," he says, claiming he only signed with Indiana to get other recruiters off his back. "Indiana never mentioned no help books wise, and I knew I needed help."

Although Indiana did offer tutoring for its athletes, just as most colleges do, Drummer eventually signed a scholarship with Gardner-Webb College, a small Baptist school in Boiling Springs, North Carolina, although he would change his mind about entering that school also.

Gardner-Webb assistant coach Roger Banks had become a father figure to Drummer, their relationship having started when Drummer was in the ninth grade. Banks, for 15 years one of the Southeast's most successful recruiters, had first seen Drummer play on a Muncie playground and had befriended him. He became the only person Drummer trusted during his recruitment.

"I thought he (Banks) was really interested in helping me," says Drummer. "I just got so hooked to him, attached to him, I don't know how to say it. I never really met no one like him. He helped me out with lots of things, advice and everything."

"Sammy was like family to us," says Banks, 39, now living in Newland, North Carolina, and working as regional director of Jim Barfield Inc., an insurance and employee-benefit company.

Drummer would later baby-sit for Banks's children and be tutored by Banks's wife, and even now Banks often uses the pronoun "we" when talking about Drummer's career.

"Nobody during Sammy's recruiting process knew of his insecurity academically," says Banks. "Sammy had a lot of pride and he didn't want anybody else to know he had those kind of [academic] problems. And nobody else that recruited him really cared [about those problems]. He was too good a player."

When Banks left Gardner-Webb during the summer of '75 and was hired at Austin Peay University, a small state-supported school in Clarksville, Tennessee, that had recently developed a strong basketball program, Drummer decided he too would go to Austin Peay. Because he had not yet enrolled at Gardner-Webb and because Gardner-Webb belonged to the National Association of Intercollegiate Athletics and Austin Peay to the NCAA, Drummer was able to receive a scholarship at Austin Peay and play that season.

Drummer planned to major in physical education at Austin Peay and about half the classes he took as a freshman were P.E. courses, according to Banks.

Drummer averaged 16.7 points per game as a freshman at Austin Peay, but when the season ended and Banks got a better-paying job at Georgia Tech, Drummer decided he would follow Banks to Atlanta.

Because of NCAA rules, Drummer could not transfer from Austin Peay to Georgia Tech without sitting out a basketball season. So he instead transferred to DeKalb South, where he did not have to miss a season, because it's a junior college and not under NCAA jurisdiction. That season he was named player of the year by the National Junior College Athletic Association, averaging 28.9 points and 13.8 rebounds a game.

To play for a senior college again, according to NCAA rules, Drummer had to graduate from DeKalb South. He totaled the necessary 90 credit hours for graduation by transferring approximately 40 hours from Austin Peay and attending DeKalb South for four quarters. Again, he had his choice of colleges, but he chose Tech to remain close to Banks.

"I told Sammy he would never graduate from Georgia Tech," says Banks, "but once he came out of Tech and into the pros, we'd get him in school somewhere else and he'd get his degree even if it took 10 years."

"Sammy was a weak student for Georgia Tech," says George Slayton, academic adviser to Tech athletes. "He had a good attitude and he went to class well but he was a very, very weak student. I am sure he felt totally out of place, because he wasn't up to the other students in academic ability. His background was very weak, but he tried at least."

Although Drummer was a junior in athletic eligibility when he entered Tech, he was able to transfer only about half his previous credits so, academically, he was the equivalent of a late freshman or early sophomore.

Asked if Drummer was put at a disadvantage by being admitted to Tech, his former coach, Dwane Morrison, says, "We were honest with every youngster that came in, telling them that it was difficult. But we were also honest in telling them the tutoring was available."

While Drummer remembers few courses he took at Tech, Banks remembers him taking some textile courses and Slayton remembers him taking some courses that he did not need as an industrial management major.

"We had to give him some free elective work because he didn't have the background to go into all the required courses he needed," says Slayton. "Sometimes you have to give the athlete things that don't count toward graduation to keep him around and give him a chance to get his feet on the ground."

As a basketball player, Drummer had no such adjustment problems. He was All-Metro Conference as a junior in 1977–78 and, as a senior, led Tech to its best record (17–9) of the 13-year period from 1972–1984. His career scoring average of 22.3 points per game is the second highest in Tech history.

Following his senior season, Drummer dropped out of Tech and awaited the annual spring draft of the National Basketball Association, where the minimum salary in 1979 was $35,000 per year and the average salary was $170,000. But instead of being a first-round draft choice, as he was predicted to be before his senior season, Drummer was not selected until the fourth round—by the Houston Rockets. They released him after a summer tryout camp, shattering his only lifetime goal.

"I didn't ever want to come home," he says. "I wanted to go off and melt or something."

Drummer had tryouts later in the summer with the San Antonio Spurs and Kansas City Kings but he was cut by them also.

Many pro scouts and coaches felt Drummer, at 6-5, was too small to play forward and not a good enough ball-handler to play guard. And wherever he tried to play, he carried the tag of a fourth-round draft pick. If he had been a first-round choice, he would have been virtually assured of making a team.

Banks believes Drummer was hurt by playing at Georgia Tech, where Morrison's deliberate offense did not showcase Drummer's running and jumping ability, only his excellent shooting skills. Banks, who left Tech to become an assistant coach at the University of Georgia before Drummer's senior season, says he made a mistake in "placing" Drummer at Tech.

Finally, in the fall of '79, Drummer got a job with the Harlem Globetrotters. He signed a $35,000 contract, but in only four months he had gone from basketball stud to basketball clown.

Then in November 1980, during his second season with the Globetrotters' international team, Drummer, along with teammate Rickey Brown, was arrested in São Paulo, Brazil, for possession of marijuana and cocaine. Drummer contends that he was "set up" by a group of Brazilians hoping to obtain a payoff from the Globetrotters and that the cocaine and marijuana were planted in his hotel room. Drummer says he has never used cocaine and only smoked marijuana in college.

Although he was never convicted, Drummer was fired by the Globetrotters and, after spending two months in a São Paulo jail, was deported to the U.S.

His future as a pro player—in the U.S. or Europe—was suddenly very dim. "There wasn't any opportunity from there on," says Banks. "There was no way you could explain it (the drug charges)."

Moving in with Banks, Drummer took a construction job in Athens. "That's something I never figured I'd be doing," he says.

Banks did get Drummer a tryout with the Hawks in the summer of '81, but he was released. Later that year Banks got Drummer a tryout in Belgium, but he didn't make that team either.

Afterward, Drummer went back to Muncie to live with his girlfriend.

Unable to find steady work in Muncie, Drummer spent a year putting roofs and siding on houses and cutting trees to sell for firewood. He got his job at Ball State (18,000 enrollment) almost two years ago when the supervisor of custodial services, Jim Frazier, made a deal with him. "He said if I played basketball on his (industrial league) team and we won the league, he'd hire me," says Drummer. "We went 13–0."

Drummer's nightly duties include dusting, sweeping, cleaning bathrooms and labs, picking up trash in vending areas, and locking up as many as a dozen buildings at the end of his shift. University Gym is one of his buildings.

Driving a van with mop buckets hanging in the back, Drummer gets a call on his beeper when a janitor is needed in his area: a professor has locked his keys in his office, there's a water leak, someone has gotten sick. "You be doing something important," says Drummer, "and some student drops a pop and you have to run over there to clean it up."

Although he smiles as often as ever, Drummer says he is bitter about the way his life has turned out. He says that if he could do it over, he would stay at one school. "Transferring so much," he says, "they (the pros) might have wondered, 'What kind of guy is this?' "

Drummer had looked forward to taking care of his family financially by playing in the NBA but says he doesn't earn enough money even to marry his girlfriend, Rosemary Baily. She has four children by a previous marriage, a fifth by Drummer, and another by Drummer on the way. He has thought about working two jobs as well as completing his degree at Ball State.

Banks believes Drummer really would like to have a college degree. "I don't think he would have paid the price to sit in class and be humiliated over and over again if he didn't," says Banks.

Drummer hasn't talked with Banks in 1½ years and has lost contact with all his other former college coaches and teammates. He says he hasn't heard from his former agent, Jack Manton of Cumming, since the arrest in Brazil.

Drummer plays basketball once a week in a Muncie industrial league at his old junior high school, plays in pickup games at Ball State on his days off, and would like to switch to the morning work shift so he would have more time to play basketball. He is unable to relinquish the dream completely.

"I haven't given up. I love the sport too much to give up just like that," he says. "I sit back and watch and deep inside of me I know I should be out there. I would like to give it one more shot."

It's not a dream Drummer necessarily holds for his children, however. He tells a story about his girlfriend's 9-year-old son, who loves to play basketball. The boy recently brought home a report card with two F's on it. Drummer was upset: "I told him, 'I'm not that smart, but I'd rather see y'all learn something than be like I am now.'"

Reprinted from Sam Heys, "Former Player Cleans Up the Gym," *Atlanta Journal-Constitution*, 1985. © With permission of the *Atlanta Journal and Constitution*, P.O. Box 4689, Atlanta, GA 30302.

"TOO STRENUOUS
FOR GIRLS"

*In the beginning, girls' basketball in Indiana was a
stepchild. Later, due to Depression economics and the
prevailing male attitude, it became no child at all. Then
came Title IX and the Liberation Seventies. When the
Indiana High School Athletic Association [IHSAA]
sponsored its first state girls' tournament in 1976,
veterans of long-ago girls' interscholastic play just
sighed. All of a sudden, after years of public noninterest,
their school-day memories were sought, marveled at,
reveled in. One of the most graphic memories was
written by Mildred Blake of Wadesville for the 1985
edition of Herb Schwomeyer's* Hoosier HERsteria. *It
follows. Mildred recalls that New Harmony refused to
play her Mt. Vernon team during the 1925–26 season
because the latter—in trunks—was "immorally clad."*

It has been with great interest that I have watched the return of interscholastic girls' basketball to the high school scene. It has a long way to go
to reach the fervor and excitement of girls' basketball in the 1920s. At that
time the girls' teams provided the first game of the evening as a sort of
"curtain raiser" for the boys' games to follow. Quite often the "curtain
raiser" provided the most exciting action of the evening. All the schools
that had a boys' team also had a girls' team. Evansville Central, Evansville
Reitz, Evansville Bosse, Boonville, Ft. Branch, Owensville, New Harmony,
Mt. Vernon, and many now-defunct high schools fielded teams. Mt. Vernon
frequently had the strongest teams in the "Pocket." More than once Mt.
Vernon claimed a "mythical" state championship with no challengers for
the title. There was no tournament system for the girls' teams.

Since there was no required physical education in those days, the
coach for the girls was merely an interested lady faculty member. Mt.
Vernon had a man coach for several years. That school's best teams were
performing during the time H.B. Allgood was guiding them. A lady faculty
member always traveled with the team as a sort of chaperone.

106

The costumes that the girls wore started out as long black bloomers (to the knees) with a white "middy" shirt complete with a scarf tie for the top. These bloomers may have been quite a help as compared with skirts, but they were usually made of a material called "sateen" that had a tendency to bunch up between the legs and more or less looked bad and felt worse. To that add long black stockings to the knee. Over the years the bloomers became skimpier and shorter. The school colors were used in many interesting fashions. Then in the mid-20s the Mt. Vernon girls were the first to appear in wool "trunks." They were longer than the boys' trunks, but in that day they were a startling innovation. I remember that many mothers weren't sure they wanted their daughters attired like that in public.

My first recollection is of a five-member team. The center, however, was the only player who covered the whole floor. The two guards and the two forwards stayed in their half of the floor. Remember that the playing floor was much smaller in those days. At some point "the powers that be" decided such activity was too strenuous for young women. Then, for only one or two seasons at the most, a nine-member team was tested. The floor was lined off in thirds, three members of each team staying within their assigned third. That really took the action out of the game. Imagine! Eighteen girls on the floor! The next try was six girls on each team. Three guards and three forwards did not cross the center line. For a time one of the guards jumped center. Later a forward was allowed to jump at the tip-off and return immediately to her side of the floor. Can you picture what the activity was like at the center line? Three girls of each team lined up, elbowing their "men" in order to snag the ball should it come even near. Needless to say, if a toe touched that center line, the owner of the toe had committed a foul.

It is hard to say just what killed girls' basketball as an interscholastic sport in the thirties. It could have been the "Great Depression" when all frills were cut out of the curriculum. It could still have then been considered too strenuous for girls. At any rate, it disappeared in the State of Indiana. Old high school annuals remain to record the story.

EMPEROR AND
DICTATOR

*The main difference between coaches and political
dictators is that the former can be more easily fired.
Like his counterparts in Indiana's basketball hotbeds,
Bill Green of perennially successful Marion is the
biggest man in town between November and April. He
runs a substantial empire, and he steers teenaged
players through annual hoopla that finds hardwood
stars, old and new, idolized more than civic leaders
and the season ticket a key item in divorce settlements.
A story by John S. Lang from a 1986 issue of*
U.S. News & World Report *tells the Marion
atmosphere.*

Bill Green is so powerful in these parts he can keep teenagers from kissing.
For five months out of every year, he can even stop them from holding
hands. In fact, from now until next spring, Bill Green's orders can affect
the behavior of practically every man, woman, and child in this factory
town of 32,000.

He's the coach.

In a state where happiness is decided on the bounces of round balls,
where tall boys in short pants are celebrities, and where two points in
the 12th grade can earn you more respect than a six-figure income in
maturity, a high school basketball coach like Bill Green is reckoned to have
and deserve almost divine rights.

Hoosiers, as people in this state call themselves, are so obsessed with
the sport that when Lebanon or Milan is in the news, they think of Rick
Mount and Bobby Plump—middle-aged men from Indiana towns of those
names whose feats on the hardwood a generation ago are still the stuff
of barroom disputes.

In Marion, 20,000 people will turn out at 1:00 A.M. to welcome home
the team that wins the state tournament. Marion High has only 2,200
pupils but needs a gym that seats 7,640 to hold the fans, many of whom
hurry home to see the action all over again on the replay telecast by the

town's religious channel. Season tickets to high school games are so valued that stubs wind up as evidence for property settlements in divorce hearings.

To make the Marion Giants, 6½-foot-tall youths in the throes of adolescent passion let a 52-year-old coach prohibit them from dating or even walking with girls in the halls. Bill Green is afraid they'll break up with their steadies, or that their girls will come to a game with some other guy, and his players' performance will suffer. "I tell them, 'Leave the loving to the coach,' " he says, adding with a grin, "and I tell them if they win the state, then they can have the pick of any girl." That is understatement.

Winning the state championship bestows lifelong honor to Hoosiers, often assuring college scholarships for the entire team and good jobs after that. Many a town in Indiana can point to some schoolboy star of once upon a time who could never bring himself to leave home and give up hero status that, one day, will get him a longer obituary than a civic leader who never played the game.

Of course, Kentucky is wild about basketball, too, and Texas is famed for hometown football, but nowhere does a high school sport seem to so define a people's sense of themselves. Why this is so goes back almost a century, to two years after basketball was invented by Dr. James Naismith. A Presbyterian minister named Nicholas McKay visited Naismith's YMCA camp in Springfield, Massachusetts, in 1893 and moved on to Indiana with a refinement. Instead of peach baskets, he had two metal hoops forged and sewed coffee sacks around them.

Right away, the game was a boon for a state of small family farms and hamlets where there was little to do after November winds browned stubble in the cornfields. Once somebody figured out the action might go faster if holes were cut in the sacks, games on Friday nights became as important as church on Sunday for bringing a community together. When somebody else devised a state tournament in which all schools, regardless of size, competed for one title, whole towns caravaned around the state to root for their teams.

The consequences were enormous for Indiana. This is a flatland that— except for the Wabash and Ohio rivers in the south—has no geography, climate, or resources to distinguish it from its Midwest neighbors. Indiana is just lines on a map. But with basketball, people here came together— and set themselves apart. And they built 18 of the 20 largest high school gyms in the U.S. and eight of the nine biggest in the world.

Hoosiers. Over the years two books with the same title, *Hoosier Hysteria*, have been written to chronicle what the game has done to these people and what they have done to the game. Now, there are a new book and a new movie, both simply named *Hoosiers*. The book, by expatriate Phillip M. Hoose, celebrates the phenomenon with wit and whimsy. In the film, Gene Hackman plays a disgraced coach who goes to Indiana and achieves personal redemption, finds true love, salvages the town drunk and takes his plowboy team to the finals. Not a bad season.

"But what really happened is too Hollywood for people to believe it," says Bob Plump. He should know, for he still gets phone calls late at night from boozy Hoosiers trying to settle a barroom bet over what he did more than three decades ago.

In 1953, Coach Marvin Wood came to Milan, population 1,000, and the next year he took a school with an enrollment of 161 and no player over 6 feet tall to the championship. Trailing by 2 points in the final quarter, Wood devised a tactic he called cat and mouse. For 4 minutes and 15 seconds, Bobby Plump just stood near center court with the ball on his hip, doing nothing. The other team, Muncie, was content to let him waste time; after all, they were leading. Coach Wood stared at the ceiling, pondering, he later confessed, what to do. Finally Plump shot. And missed! As the clock wound down, Milan stole the ball and evened the score, stole the ball again, and moved ahead. Then, with 18 seconds left, Muncie retied the game, 30–30. Coach Wood sent four Milan players to one side of the court, drawing off the Muncie team, leaving Plump to go one-on-one. Just before the buzzer, he tried a jumper. Next morning the *Indianapolis Star* led the front page with a picture of the ball frozen above the hoop and a one-word headline: "Plump."

To find a local legend as big as Plump, go way back, almost to when games were played in churches and boys arced shots through the rafters, or in taverns where they banked balls off ceilings, or in chicken-wire cages so the ball stayed in play. In 1920, 1921, and 1922, Franklin's high school became the only one to win the state title back-to-back-to-back. That team, all dead today, is still renowned as the Wonder Five.

And now Bill Green is poised to match that 65-year-old record. He has won more state titles—five—than any other coach. He won in 1985 and 1986, and he's coming back in 1987 with the same starters—two already signed by Indiana University, one by Wake Forest, and another sure to be grabbed by a Division I college. All have played together since they were seven years old.

Green has a sports empire that would be the envy of any college. He bosses every coach of every boys' team in every school in Marion. His afternoons are free to drop in on the practices of seventh and eighth-grade squads. He boasts a tout sheet, much like those for racehorses, on every one of the 125 boys who play basketball for Marion schools: "Every year coaches write personality reports on each kid. We know what size shoes they wear, how tall their parents are. This sheet travels with him until he gets to varsity level."

Growing up in Green's system is no surety of making the team. Some years ago he cut his own son from the squad after deciding the boy wasn't a good enough shooter. "Broke his heart," says Green. "He didn't speak to me for two weeks." Pause. "If I had it to do over again, I'd a kept him."

He believes it, but it probably isn't so. Winning at basketball means so much to Green that he took a $20,000 pay cut to come back to coaching after going into business. And losing is unbearable. His first years at Marion he lost the sectional play-offs. "They egged my house. Waitresses were slow to take my order. Only kept my job by one vote of the school board, 4 to 5."

If Marion wins its third straight title at the state finals next March 29, Green can have any position here he wants—"be mayor, run on any kind of ticket. It's been offered before." But if he loses? "Hoosiers," he sighs, "they're always long on spirit, but sometimes short on memory. They're 100 percent with you—win or tie. Of course, in basketball there is no tie."

GYMLESS WONDERS

*It's hard to imagine a more popular champion than
Wingate or one easier to write about. The little
Montgomery County school, with a male enrollment
of 12, no gym, and nondescript uniforms, won two
consecutive Indiana state championships just before
World War I. A few years later another Wingate team
won the national tournament in Chicago. When the
school finally got a gym, it was a barn-looking
structure, seating 187 and heated by potbellied stoves
in the corners. Compared with Wingate, even Milan
was large and upscale.*

It's futile to compare athletes separated by several generations, particularly
in basketball where changes in rules, tempo, technique, and player size
have been so great. One judges an athlete against his peers. If he's a
teenage equivalent of Ruth, Dempsey, or Grange, his exploits will survive
the ages, perhaps swell with them, and he'll become a fixture on everybody's all-time all-star team. Once a fixture, he is hard to dislodge.

Such a player was Homer Stonebraker, the star of tiny Wingate's back-
to-back state champions in 1913 and 1914 and later a three-time all-America
at Wabash College down the road in Crawfordsville. A big enforcer with
great inside moves, Stonebraker was an all-around player who could hit
consistently from distance—in an era when careless nonpercentage shooting meant automatic benching if not lengthy suspension. As a tall guy
often performing in low-ceilinged gyms, he perfected a low-trajectory long
shot with backspin that would strike the backboard and plop in.

Stonebraker's aura has been enhanced by the overall Wingate saga.
With no gym during the 1912–13 season, Coach Jesse Wood and his charges
traveled six miles to New Richmond for practice. Victories that 22-victory
season include 108–8 over Hillsboro, 85–9 over Cayuga, 75–7 over Waveland,
and 60–5 over Covington. Against the big boys in the Indiana University
gym, they defeated Whiting, 24–12; Rochester, 19–17 in overtime; Indianapolis Manual, 16–11; and Lafayette Jefferson, 23–14; then, in a memorable game, nipped South Bend Central, 15–14, in *five* two-minute overtimes. Stonebraker, the center, had 9 of the 15, and forward Forest Crane,

whose field goal won the marbles for Wingate, registered the other 6. Other team regulars were forward Leland Olin and guards John Graves and John Blacker.

Team uniforms that season consisted of baseball trousers, long socks, and sweatshirts. Sometimes the team practiced outdoors, with hoops nailed to posts. Coach Wood and the players made the trip to the Crawfordsville sectional in two Model T taxis, then rode a Monon train to Bloomington for the state finals.

Things tightened up a bit in the 1913–14 campaign, but Stonebraker was back, along with Olin, Graves, and Blacker. Lee Sinclair, a reserve from 1912–13, replaced the graduated Crane, and Wingate, under new coach Leonard Lehman, fashioned a 19–5 record. At Bloomington the team was required to play two games on Friday—44–14 over Milan and 44–12 over Westport—and *four* on Saturday. In the final-day triumphs Wingate allowed only 7.5 points a game. In an 8:00 A.M. game perennial rival Crawfordsville was crushed, 24–1. In the afternoon Clinton and Lebanon were outlasted, 17–13 and 14–8, respectively, with Stonebraker accounting for all 17 Wingate points in the former encounter. By the night final, Stonebraker and mates were under a full head of steam. They routed mighty Anderson, 36–8, with Stonebraker accounting for 18 points, more than twice the foe's entire production. A newcomer reserve on this squad was Pete Thorn, who would later win 16 letters in four sports at Wabash College, play on that school's national intercollegiate championship team in 1922, and in 1940 be named by the *Indianapolis News* as the greatest athlete in Wabash history.

Today's proselytizing of athletes apparently differs from early-day practice only in degree. This isn't and wasn't just a college thing as a 1920 scenario reveals. Both Wingate and Crawfordsville would have been major state title contenders that year. Wingate had Alonzo Goldsberry, a worthy successor to Stonebraker and Thorn. But both schools were under IHSAA suspension for using ineligible players and other reasons. One of the counts against Crawfordsville was using undue influence in contacting Goldsberry. The suspensions did not deter the University of Chicago from inviting both teams to its second National Interscholastic tournament. The Hoosier schools met in the final, Wingate prevailing, 22–16, and further cementing the name of a now-defunct school in state and national annals. In early rounds the champions downed teams from Iowa, Ohio, and Illinois. Goldsberry was named captain of the all-tournament squad.

Wingate played its last game in 1953. The school was consolidated out of existence, and the community is now part of the North Montgomery High School system. But legends linger. Hoosier historians believe the term "barnburner," meaning a tight, exciting game, had its origin in the Wingate "barn," site of home games from 1915 on.

Predictably Stonebraker was elected to the Indiana Basketball Hall of Fame in the year of its founding, 1962. His fellow pioneer electees were

John Wooden, Ward "Piggy" Lambert, R.F. "Fuzzy" Vandivier, and Ernest "Griz" Wagner, each a household name among Hoosier basketball aficionados. Stonebraker is also on the most frequently published all-time Indiana "dream team." Based on high school play only, the lineup reads:

Oscar Robertson (Indianapolis Crispus Attucks '56)
Fuzzy Vandivier (Franklin '22)
George McGinnis (Indianapolis Washington '69)
John Wooden (Martinsville '28)
Homer Stonebraker (Wingate '14)

By the early twenties, Indiana was recognized as the nation's basketball hub. Wabash was the nation's top college team. Stonebraker was Wabash's best player. Ergo Stonebraker was frequently if not generally or justifiably regarded as the best basketball player in America. He was the Oscar Robinson and Larry Bird of his day.

"Could any of those old-timers really cut it with the modern fast-breaking teams?" veteran Hoosier basketball watchers have been asked a hundred times. Usually there is brief silence, then a few names tumble out. Invariably there is agreement on three—Wooden, Vandivier, and, yes, Stonebraker.

TRIBUTE

Not all coaches are saints or even role models, but many of them are. The most memorable of Indiana's particularly distinguished group of high school basketball mentors were those who held the fort during the dark days of the Depression. Often poorly paid but unusually dedicated, they imparted values that served their charges well on the battlefields of war and life. There were Cliff Wells, Marion Crawley, Everett Case, Glenn Curtis, Archie Chadd, and Burl Friddle among others. There was also Raymond "Pete" Jolly of Muncie Central whose teams played in three state finals, won two of them, and averaged 20 victories a season over 13 years. After Jolly's death in 1981, sports editor Bob Barnet of the Muncie Star *wrote the following tribute. It also appeared in* Hoosier Hysteria!, *authored by Bob Williams of the* Indianapolis Star *and published a year later by Icarus Press.*

Once again the bell has tolled, and Pete Jolly is gone.

His sudden passing on Christmas Day took another of those teacher-coaches whose strength and determination helped Hoosiers fight on during the grim years of the Great Depression and in World War II.

Through the late 1920s, the decade of the Thirties, and the first few years of the 1940s they taught young men—and their families—that life is often hard but victory over adversity can be achieved if hearts are stout and men and women possess the will to try again.

On basketball court and football field and in the arenas of other sports they taught by word and example that victory is better than defeat as long as it is fairly and honorably won and that defeat comes to all humans and must be accepted with grace and dignity.

By helping make it possible for Indiana high schools to offer low-cost entertainment of exceptional quality and strong appeal, they helped lift the spirits of families pounded by a terrible depression. Often it was the only entertainment available.

When the great war came many of these coaches and their athletes went away to fight their nation's battles. Their performances in this most demanding of all competitions proved that they, as athletes, had learned lessons vital to their survival and that of their homeland.

Indiana high school basketball in those years was in the hands of a race of giants and Raymond (Pete) Jolly stood as tall as any man. Nearly all of them, and surely Jolly, came from working families of the type hit hardest by depression. They knew what it meant to do without things and knew that athletes who sometimes tired in practice were weary because they were hungry.

Nearly all these coaches were college graduates and teachers because they had earned a measure of assistance as athletes. They were grateful for what athletics had done for them.

Jolly had served in the U.S. Navy during World War I, then returned to New Castle High School because Frank E. Allen, the New Castle principal and later superintendent of Muncie schools, convinced him that a man needed to complete high school and go to college. At Purdue the young Jolly had played varsity football and basketball. Allen died recently at the age of 90 and Jolly said of his older leader: "Everything I have, everything I am, I owe to him."

Basketball was a careful game, a game of tactics, a chess game when Pete Jolly coached. The run-and-shoot game was practiced by only a few like Murray Mendenhall of Fort Wayne Central. Other coaches ran only when they had players with great speed and the ball-handling skill to match.

These coaches of the 1930s and early forties planned carefully for every game but always "the tournament" was their goal.

Pete coached through the era of the stall game and in the stands nerves were drawn tight because a single shot, a single basket, meant so much in this type of play.

To those who followed the Bearcats—and that included all Muncie residents except those who cheered for Burris, the only other school in town—one of the greatest thrills in sport came when Pete Jolly rose from the bench, took a step toward the sideline, and sent his purpleclads storming downcourt with a single wave of his right hand.

Spectators came up screaming. The coach was tired of watching that other team hold the ball. The Bearcats were going after them!

Pete Jolly was a great coach. More important, he was an honest, honorable man, a good teacher, a friend who always had time to help a high-schooler look for a summer job in those depression years.

He and his lovely Doris were among Muncie's best-liked, most-respected citizens in the years they lived among us.

From *Hoosier Hysteria!*, published by the Icarus Press, Inc. Copyright © 1982 by Bob Williams. Reprinted with permission.

INDIANA POTPOURRI

*Superlatives, oddities, and memorable anecdotes
collected over the years from Indiana*

When Coach Larry Steele brought his 1989–90 University of Portland team
east to play Butler in Indianapolis and Kentucky in Lexington, he experienced nostalgia in huge doses. Twenty-two years earlier he had led little
Bainbridge to Indiana's Final Eight, and in the ensuing seasons he had
starred at Kentucky.

The memories of Bainbridge, 35 miles from Indianapolis down Highway 36, ran deepest. With Larry scoring and stealing all over the court,
his Pointers were about to overtake mighty Lafayette Jefferson in the semistate when Jefferson's revered coach, Marion Crawley, stepped onto the
floor. Jefferson had run out of time-outs, but no technical was called. Bainbridge partisans still ponder what might have happened if the opposing
coach had been anyone except the immortal Crawley.

Back in Bainbridge a generation later, Larry drove by the barn door
where he first shot at an old bent rim. Bainbridge High School was torn
down to make way for a school bus shed, and the district was absorbed
into North Putnam High at Roachdale. Thus much of the identity is gone.
So is the old gym. But memories of Larry and his mates in a crackerbox
gym, with five rows of bleachers on each side and a stage at one end,
live on. You can always find a few townsfolk who will replay that
Bainbridge-Jefferson game for you.

During the filming of *Hoosiers*, loosely based on little Milan's 1954 championship trail, it took Jimmy Chitwood 10 takes to get the winning Bobby
Plump shot just right. To achieve proper camera angles production people
had to move 5,000 spectators around to different sections of the field house.

After the Athens Hornets of Texas won their second straight national interscholastic championship in 1930, Coach Jimmie Kitts lamented the absence
of an Indiana team in the event. At this point in history, the IHSAA pro-
hibited participation by its schools, and Kitts was quoted as saying he
wished he could "show" Hoosierdom, too, how the game is played.

117

Several Indiana prep coaches got together to help him out. Knowing most of Kitts's team would return, they arranged a nine-game Hoosier schedule for Athens during the next Christmas holiday season. It was a disaster for the Hornets. They defeated only Brazil and Horace Mann of Gary while losing to Martinsville (by 24 points), Frankfort (by 16), Shelbyville (by 15), Lafayette Jefferson, Evansville Central, Washington, and New Albany.

Dick and Tom Van Arsdale were born 15 minutes apart and would leave an amazing trail of parallel basketball achievements. Dick grew to 6-4½ and 210, Tom to 6-5 and 215. They led Indianapolis Manual to second place in the 1961 state tournament, shared "Mr. Basketball" and Trester Award honors, completed three-year varsity careers with 16.3 and 15.7 averages, respectively, and graduated first and third in their class.

At Indiana University they were even closer carbon copies. Tom totaled 1,252 points to Dick's 1,240 and posted a razor-thin rebounding margin, 723–719. Both made the all-Big 10 second team, they shared all-conference MVP honors, and both made the NCAA's academic all-America. In long NBA careers Dick averaged 16.4 points in 921 games, Tom 15.3 in 929 games. They were together only one year in the pros—at Phoenix in 1976–77 when they were 34 years old.

When Greg Bell, a Butler University student from metropolitan Buffalo, New York, told the home folks in 1971 that many regular-season high school basketball games in Indiana draw more than 7,500 fans, are heavily covered by newspapers and TV, and are broadcast by radio, they didn't believe him. How could a high school game draw 7,500 fans? Surely the listing that the New Castle High field house seated 9,325 was a mistake.

At that time New York high schools had no state tournament. When the 18-game season ended, they simply got ready for baseball. The team at Bell's 3,200-student school averaged about 500 fans and received virtually no media coverage. Bell, who would become sports director at WIOU in Kokomo, had found a new love.

Joe Dean, the onetime New Albany and LSU star, now athletic director at his college alma mater, vainly tries to explain the Indiana magic to listeners far away. "You mean they get that excited over a *high school* game?" they ask in wonderment. "You have to live there to understand," Dean counters.

Girls' interscholastic basketball in Indiana, as we know it, began in 1976, but yellowed documents reveal considerable competition before the Depression quashed the activity.

The Wabash High Snowballs compiled an awesome record in the freelancing twenties, claiming the 1929 "state title" on the basis of a 14–0 record that included two decisive postseason triumphs over Argos, "the only other contender." The Snowballs followed with season records of 12-1-1 in 1929-30, then 10-0-1 in 1930-31, with only Auburn spoiling the streak. They claimed a world record with a 122-1 slaughtering of a newly organized Fairmount team on the latter's home floor. The ball was in hapless Fairmount's half of the floor only five times. Charlotte Engle of the 1928-29 Snowballs won individual honors at the state free throwing contest, sinking 47 out of 50.

Six decades are represented among Indiana's 10 most resounding Final 16 upsets, as cited by Herb Schwomeyer, dean of the state's basketball historians. In chronological order they are:

1931—Rushville 21, Gary Horace Mann 20
1932—Cicero 17, Vincennes 15
1935—Anderson 23, Jeffersonville 17
1947—Shelbyville 68, Terre Haute Garfield 58
1954—Milan 32, Muncie Central 30
1960—East Chicago Washington 75, Muncie Central 59
1965—Fort Wayne North 74, Gary Roosevelt 65
1976—Rushville 68, East Chicago Washington 59
1977—Carmel 53, East Chicago Washington 52
1982—Plymouth 75, Gary Roosevelt 74 (two OTs)

In 1938 a snowstorm blocked most of the roads in southern Indiana, and 350 Jeffersonville fans were forced to spend the night in Indiana University's Assembly Hall. They slept on the court and in the wrestling room. In 1965 a 12-inch snow and 50-mile-an-hour winds caused postponement of games at 57 of Indiana's 64 sectionals.

Butlerville High successfully used a "squirrel stunt" three times during the 1922-23 season—against Scipio, Hayden, and Vernon. A 5-foot, 110-pound Butlerville forward named Merlin Swarthout would fake his guard out of position, scramble up the back of bent-over 6-4 center Raymond Rees, take a quick pass, and lay the ball in the basket. The ploy against Vernon occurred in the final moments of a sectional semifinal and gave Butlerville a 16-15 victory. At the time there was nothing in the rules against the "squirrel," but it was never used again, not even in the sectional final, which Butlerville lost to Seymour. The next year a rule prohibiting "squirrel" type assistance was enacted.

Among the many obstacles the all-black schools had to surmount in the early days of integration into the IHSAA was scheduling. Crispus Attucks of Indianapolis, for example, had no suitable gym prior to 1966. Years went by before a game with an Indianapolis black school would be a profitable venture in an outstate community. In the interim it was difficult to schedule games with strong teams. What school wanted a probable loss both on the scoreboard and at the gate?

But legendary coach Howard Sharpe of Terre Haute Gerstmeyer put Crispus Attucks on his schedule, and that paved the way. Attucks partisans never forgot the gesture. When Oscar Robertson was inducted into the Indiana Basketball Hall of Fame in 1982, 11 years after Sharpe, he paid special tribute to the latter for breaking the ice.

History has recorded at least one tie game in Indiana. The year was 1936, and the opponents were Indianapolis Tech and the eventual state champion Frankfort Hog Dogs. It was 31–all at the end of regulation time. After two overtimes failed to break the deadlock, the coaches—Bayne Freeman of Tech and legendary Everett Case of Frankfort—agreed to call things off, a prerogative then permitted. Thus Frankfort's season record became 29-1-1.

Case's high school record at Columbus, Smithfield, Anderson, and Frankfort wound up at 726-75-1 and his overall an incredible 1,161-214-1, including 18 years at North Carolina State and a stint at DePauw Navy Pre-Flight. The old master died in 1966. He left an estate valued at $201,125, of which $5,000 was bequeathed to a North Carolina State scholarship fund and $1,000 to Frankfort High School, with the balance divided among 57 of his former players.

Picturesque team nicknames in Indiana include several of historical, mythological, or occupational connotation. They include the Delphi Oracles, New Harmony Rappites, Garrett Railroaders, River Forest Ingots, Plymouth Pilgrims, Tell City Marksmen, Speedway Sparkplugs, Whiting Oilers, Crawfordsville Athenians, Concord Minutemen, and Roosevelt (East Chicago) Rough Riders.

Other creative Hoosier nicknames are the Logansport Berries, Martinsville Artesians, Rochester Zebras, Mishawawka Cavemen, Shoals Jug Rox, Pendleton Heights Arabians, Rising Sun Shiners, Madison Grant (Fairmount) Argylls, Lincoln (Vincennes) Alices, Wabash Apaches, South Adams Starfires, Northeast Dubois Jeeps, Manchester Squires, and South Union Satellites.

It wasn't until 1957 that the Indiana High School Athletic Association's Board of Control gave official recognition to the 1911 state tournament.

That 12-team event was conducted by the Indiana University Boosters Club in the Assembly Hall after the board, believing the plan unworkable, refused to sanction it. One team was to have been invited from each of the state's 13 congressional districts, but the number was reduced to 12 when the Indianapolis school board would not permit Manual or Short-ridge to participate. Crawfordsville won the championship, defeating Lebanon, 24–17.

In what may have been the greatest single-game individual scoring duel of all time, Ray Pavy of New Castle outshot Jimmy Rayl of Kokomo, 51–49, on February 20, 1959. Host New Castle won the North Central Conference game, 92–81. Pavy and Rayl entered Indiana University together, became roommates, and played together. Rayl became a Big 10 all-star, but tragedy struck Pavy just before the start of his junior year. He suffered a paralyzing injury in a collision on Highway 41 in northwest Indiana. From a wheel-chair he coached successfully at Shenandoah, Middletown, and Sulphur Springs before entering administration in his hometown.

All-America University of Illinois quarterback Jeff George was a three-sport athlete at Warren Central High School in Indianapolis. As such, he received a unique award prior to a February 28, 1986, basketball game at Greenfield Central. It was an engraved clock, presented on behalf of the student body of the *opposing school!* The Greenfield people congratulated George on his achievements at Warren Central and wished him well in college. The presentation was capped by a standing ovation.

Few cities under 200,000 can match the broad distribution of Fort Wayne's five state and national championships. Three different Fort Wayne high schools—South (1938 and 1958), Central (1943), and Northrup (1974)—have won boys' state titles while Central Catholic captured back-to-back national Catholic crowns in 1939 and 1940.

In 1948 Jeffersonville coach Ed Denton called 17 time-outs during his team's winning effort against Henryville in the first afternoon semifinal game of the home sectional. The presumed objective was to shorten the rest period for the winner of the second semifinal, which turned out to be New Albany. The ploy failed. New Albany won the night final anyway, 53–31, and the IHSAA reprimanded Denton for "unsportsmanlike conduct." It also reprimanded the officials.

You can't measure high school team quality or chemistry by how well its members perform at the college level, but it's an intriguing index.

Try Crispus Attucks's 1955 champions (31–1), who won the title game by 23 points and sent Oscar Robertson to the University of Cincinnati, the NBA, and the Hall of Fame; Willie Merriweather to Purdue where he broke scoring records; Sheddrick Mitchell and Bill Scott to Butler; and Bill Hampton to Indiana Central. Crispus Attucks's 1955 accomplishments shine brightest when one learns that its victims in the finale included Dick Barnett, later a regular on the New York Knicks, and Wilson Eison, later a starter at Purdue.

Or try East Chicago Washington's 1971 champions (29–0), who won their title game by 10 points, then sent Junior Bridgeman to Louisville and the NBA, Pete Trgovich to UCLA's NCAA winners, Pete Stoddard to North Carolina State's NCAA titlists (and major league baseball), Ruben Bailey to Montana State, and Darnell Adell, later Washington's coach, to Murray State.

Take your pick. Or feel free to vote for Indianapolis Washington's 1969 juggernaut (31–0), led by the state's all-time best 1–2 frontline punch: George McGinnis and Steve Downing.

Wingate was Indiana's basketball darling before and after World War I. Milan (1954) is the all-time darling and the one whose legend has wandered farthest. Their counterpart of the seventies and eighties was little Argos, a Marshall County town of 1,500 population and 247 enrollment. En route to a state record 76 consecutive regular-season victories, the Dragons were 28–0 when they reached the Final Four in 1979. Along the way they had eliminated 1978 state finalist Elkhart Central, Fort Wayne Harding, and high-ranked Marion. Even *Sports Illustrated* covered the phenomenon, now called "The Spirit of 76" in local annals.

In 1973 the *losing* team, Anderson, scored 95 points in a state tournament semifinal game against South Bend Adams. In 1918, five and a half decades earlier, Bloomington was held scoreless from the field in another semi-final—against eventual champion Lebanon. Four free throws by Gimbel Award winner Ralph Esarey represented all the losers' scoring in a 17–4 setback. Coached by Hall of Fame selectee-to-be Cliff Wells, Bloomington bounced back to take all the marbles a year later.

Few families have compiled the credentials of the Shepherds of Indiana. Bill led Hope to the semistate in 1945, played at Butler, coached at two high schools, and was elected to the Indiana Basketball Hall of Fame in

1975. Oldest son Billy was all-state at Carmel in 1967 and 1968. Middle son Dave led Carmel to runner-up honors in 1970, pouring in 40 points in the final against East Chicago Roosevelt. Youngest son Steve was a member of Carmel's 1977 championship team.

LaTaunya Pollard, East Chicago Roosevelt '79, is on just about everybody's all-time all-America teams—at both high school and college levels. In four prep seasons she averaged 18.3 points, led her team to two state titles (1977 and 1979) while savoring a 91–2 record, and was honored as "Miss Basketball" in 1979. At Cal State Long Beach she was a three-time all-America, averaging 23.4 points over 128 games, scoring 48 in her best effort, and earning the Margaret Wade Trophy as "the nation's outstanding women's collegiate basketball player" in 1979.

While Indiana has long been generally regarded as the hottest of America's basketball hotbeds, the game did not always enjoy such widespread affection among Hoosiers. The following commentary appeared in *Arbutus*, the Indiana University yearbook, in 1911:

> *Basket-ball is systematic indoor rough house. It is played by two teams of five invalids each. Now and then a normal person is permitted to enter a basket-ball battle, but it is always because he is possessed of unusual agility or because there is a scarcity of invalids.*
>
> *The aim in basket-ball is to get a round spherical mass of leather-incased air into a butterfly net. The unreasonableness of the whole thing is that the butterfly net is without any kind of bottom, and the leather-incased air falls out as soon as it is put in. If a good butterfly net could be used, and if it could be hermetically sealed as soon as the ball is dropped in, there would be some excuse for all the struggle.*
>
> *Basket-ball, however, has many redeeming features. When a performer slips, there are only nine men and an umpire to step on his face instead of twenty-one men and a referee as in football.*

It's easy to mount a philosophical argument against high school all-star games. Some of them are mere commercial promotions. All are clearinghouses for recruiters. In how many locales can you generate spectator interest for basketball in the summertime? A big exception is the Indiana-Kentucky rivalry that goes back to 1939. Its format is now two games a year: home and away, boys and girls. At this writing the Indiana boys hold a 52–31 victory edge. Its girls are ahead, 17–11.

Seldom is a state final so epic that it inspires poetry immediately after the fact. But Milan's David-Goliath victory over Muncie Central in 1954, forever rhapsodized in boardrooms, bars, and sewing circles throughout Indiana, qualifies easily. The 20-line verse below was written by Bill Fox, Jr., of the *Indianapolis News*, himself a Hoosier legend. It appeared in Monday editions, a day and a half after the Saturday night heroics. It will never make poetry anthologies, but remember that Wordsworth and Longfellow didn't have newspaper deadlines to meet and that even veteran reporters get sentimental under the right circumstances.

> *The miracle has taken place; the little town has won—*
> *Milan-ium has touched the golden years.*
> *The multitude is now convinced; the doubters join the fun;*
> *The rafters of the fieldhouse ring with cheers.*
> *Courageously the runners-up step forward with a smile*
> *Their silver rings to take with heavy heart.*
> *The penalty of leadership upon them all the while*
> *Was more than they could bear—they now depart.*
> *The stage is left to Milan and its brilliant coach, Marv Wood,*
> *To the players who have won that title game.*
> *Triumphant now before the throng the happy heroes stood*
> *To reap the golden harvest of their fame.*
> *No victory more perfect could one possibly conceive.*
> *As one lad said, "It all seems like a dream."*
> *The words of Milan's Tiny Hunt I'm sure we all believe,*
> *"They did it, friend, because they were a team."*
> *Congratulations, Woody boy, to you and all your men—*
> *In villages and towns now skies are blue.*
> *The glory of the little town you've given us again;*
> *The hope that springs eternal's born anew.*

PART III

KENTUCKY

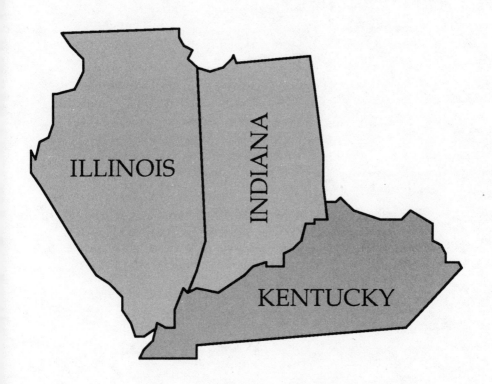

HILLS OF COAL,
FEATS OF CLAY

*We don't read much about rural poverty. The people
live far apart, they're seldom organized, and in the
mountains they're almost invisible to the media and
general public. When your economy is based on coal,
as it has been in Clay County, Kentucky, the outlook
can be particularly bleak. Clay County High School in
Manchester (population 1,600) won the Kentucky boys'
title in 1987 and was ranked among the nation's top 10
prep teams during the following season. In the process
a band of teenagers resurrected pride throughout an
entire region. They stirred the legends of Carr Creek,
Inez, and Hindman out of the taller hills a little
farther east, as well as the exploits of Kelly Coleman,
Johnny Cox, and Wallace "Wah Wah" Jones. To a
precious few, basketball can be a ticket out of the
hollow just as it is out of the city ghetto. Sam Heys's
1988 story from the* Atlanta Journal-Constitution,
*which follows, tells how a successful basketball team
became a source of hope in an area where a major
mine went bankrupt and the chief crop was marijuana.
It was adjudged the best sports feature story that
year by* The Sporting News.

The Farmer brothers learned their basketball on the side of a mountain. On
a dusty, rocky patch of earth sprinkled with small black chunks of coal.
Their shots were shadowed by an ugly, barren 40-foot-high cliff, left behind
decades ago by a coal company that did a little strip mining and moved.

Such "high walls" dot the landscape of eastern Kentucky, creating
beneath them bits of flatland rarely big enough for a factory, but always
big enough for basketball.

Richie and Russ Farmer played their basketball whenever they could:
early summer mornings, days the wind gusted relentlessly through the

127

mountains, by the light of the moon. They now play it for the vindication of Clay County.

For a county long on illiteracy and hard times and short on quality of life and high school graduates, the Farmer brothers and three other mountain boys are dishing out a little poetic justice. "Everybody thinks people from the mountains are dumb hicks, that we can't do anything," said Richie Farmer in thick mountain English. "But we can play basketball."

Indeed. Only one of its five starters is at least six feet tall—and he's only 6-foot-1—yet Clay County High School is ranked among the top 10 high school teams in America. For two years, they have been the best team in Kentucky, one of America's foremost hoops states, and their leader, Richie Farmer, is a lock to become Mr. Basketball in Kentucky at season's end.

But what the Farmers and their friends have done transcends county lines. They have uplifted an entire region: the mountains of eastern Kentucky, a pocket of isolation with little to cheer about.

Even its basketball, long the pride of the mountains, had hit hard times.

When Clay County won the state championship last year, it became the first mountain team to do so in 31 years. It did it by winning the "Sweet 16" state tournament, which annually throws both large and small schools—Clay County has a senior class of 220—into a battle royal for the kingdom of Kentucky basketball.

Clay County coach Bobby Keith, an old mountain boy himself, put it in perspective at that time: "Sometimes people in the mountains have it a little bit harder than other people, and sometimes it's kind of hard to find enough things to be proud of. But this should take care of that for a while."

The Tigers are expected to give the mountains a second dose of pride this month by becoming the first team in 17 years to win back-to-back "Sweet 16" titles. They had won 38 straight games against Kentucky teams going into the district tournament, and if they win this week's Region 13 tournament, they will enter the state tournament at Louisville on March 16 as the team to beat. They have been ranked Number 1 in Kentucky since November and are essentially the same team that won the state last year.

They are more than a team from the mountains, however; they are a mountain team. "When you talk about being a mountain team, people think of a team that tries to outhustle the other team," said Richie Farmer, "although they might be as talented."

"We want to win it for all the 5-10 and 5-11 guys that their high school coaches said were too small to play," said Keith after winning the state championship last year. "We want to prove them wrong."

The four players who have been the core of both this year's and last year's teams—the Farmers, Kevin Jackson, and Russell Chadwell—are all 5-foot-11.

"Last year the other teams looked at us and just laughed," said Chadwell, an 18-year-old senior who precedes each home game by throwing down a variety of slam dunks in pregame warm-ups.

Richie Farmer, 18, is Clay County's leader. He averages 27 points per game—his brother, a junior, averages 17—and played in his first "Sweet 16" as an eighth grader. He has a 3.8 grade-point average and is a mature, nearly flawless floor leader.

Unlike Richie Farmer, who is being courted by countless colleges, Jackson, 18, has been promised a miner's job by a Clay County coal company when he graduates this spring. One of 10 children, Jackson has handled the family farm since his father was disabled. He married a high school sophomore last summer and now tends his own farm also.

Stanley Abner, a 54-year-old coal miner's son who teaches algebra and tends the score book and public address system at Clay County games, understands clearly what the Farmers, Jackson, Chadwell, and 6-foot-1 junior Eugene Rawlings—the other starter on the 14-player roster—are accomplishing. "This just shows us what we can accomplish if we take the talent God gave us and use it," he said. "These guys are nothing but a bunch of overachievers. And Bobby Keith is the epitome of the work ethic."

Keith's favorite restaurant, Bob and Skyler's Steak House, opens at 4:30 every morning. "We miss a lot of business because we don't open any earlier," said owner Skyler Garrison. "Then they say we're sorry and won't work." The work ethic? When Wal-Mart opened in the county seat of Manchester four and a half years ago with 76 jobs, there were more than 800 applications the first day.

Clay County's unemployment rate is listed at 14 percent but most county officials put it between 30 and 35 percent. "That's about 20 percent who've never worked and there's no record on," said County Judge Executive Carl "Crawdad" Sizemore, one of a myriad of Sizemores whose political fiefdom is Clay County.

The walls of Sizemore's office on Courthouse Hill, above downtown Manchester, are decked with pictures of previous Clay County basketball teams. He talks quickly about the Sunday last March when the Tigers paraded home with the state championship. Cars lined both sides of the Daniel Boone Parkway for the 12 miles from the county line into Manchester. "I was amazed at how they lined up out of those creeks and hollows, people who may have never come to a game," he said.

Charles Marcum, who lives in the hollow below the Farmers, has missed only two of the 25 games Clay County has played in Kentucky this season. He has followed the Tigers around the state despite having to rise each morning at 3:30 for the one-and-a-half-hour trip to his job in a Harlan County coal mine. Because there is little coal mining in Clay County, now Marcum accepts his daily three-hour round trip over winding roads—as well as the three months he was out of work last year—stoically. Seeing his alma mater vanquish all obstacles on the basketball court makes his own hurdles easier to bear. "To me, this is the best thing ever to happen to Clay County, other than coal," said Marcum, 28.

Clay County is a slave to coal. The doorway to the high school gym is the escape hatch for a people who relish seeing the world shrunk to a hardwood rectangle less than 90 feet long and 50 feet wide. There, no one beats Clay County.

Off the court, Clay County has taken a beating of late:

Just two years ago, Clay County was ranked 119th out of 120 Kentucky counties in quality of life. The ratings, compiled by an Eastern Kentucky University professor, were computed from education levels, average income, crime rate, and farmland value.

The county's biggest factory, Mid-South Electrics Inc., with more than 300 employees, was destroyed by fire two and a half years ago. Its owners are rebuilding it in neighboring Jackson County, the only county Clay topped in "quality of life."

The Hardly Able Coal Company has been dragged through the courts and national news media throughout the 1980s. The Manchester-based strip-mining operation—which pumped $600,000 per month into the local economy annually and had 125 employees—is bankrupt because of the more than $500,000 it has received in federal fines for mining violations.

The county has received statewide publicity as a marijuana-growing hotbed. County officials readily admit marijuana is Clay County's Number 1 cash crop.

A legacy of violence has shrouded the county since its leading families got into a nine-year, murderous shooting feud at the turn of the century.

Family lines still run deep in Clay County. Keith believes 99 percent of the people living in the county were born there. In 18 years as coach, he has had only two players who were not sons of natives. And they were brothers.

Four of Keith's first six players are the sons of former Clay County High School players. They grew up playing basketball with their fathers, coming to Clay County games and dreaming of being a Tiger. "They want to be better than their daddies," said Keith, 47.

When Keith went to a county elementary school last spring to show off the five-and-a-half-foot-high trophy, a first grader approached him. "He said, 'When I get as big as that trophy, I'm going to play for you,' " Keith said.

Clay County's nine elementary schools—with names such as Horse Creek, Goose Rock, and Burning Springs—run through the eighth grade and usually draw a couple of hundred fans to their basketball games. The countywide tournament fills the 2,500-seat high school gymnasium.

"They get to relating to these kids, and they get attached to them," said Skyler Garrison, who coached the Tigers in the 1960s and is one of the co-owners of the embattled Hardly Able Coal Company. His restaurant is the site of a daily, impromptu roundtable basketball discussion. Old men sip coffee and compare Richie Farmer to the best guard ever to emerge from the mountains: Jerry West of West Virginia.

It was 60 years ago this season that basketball became a lifeline to the mountains of Kentucky, as the rest of the state and then America learned of the Carr Creek community of Knott County. About 200 people lived there, and 15 of them went to the high school that was perched on the side of a mountain. The basketball team had neither uniforms nor a gym. It practiced outside and traveled to its games by a mule-drawn log wagon or by foot.

In the finals of the 1928 state tournament, Carr Creek battled Ashland through four overtimes, finally losing 13–11. The Creekers went on to a national tournament in Chicago, where they became the darlings of the fans. They won two games and headed home. The mountains stood a little taller upon their return.

Finally, eastern Kentucky had a court upon which it could compete with the outside world. Mountain schools were poor and tiny, but basketball required little money, not much land, and few players. By the 1940s, mountain schools were dominating Kentucky basketball.

Keith was born in 1940. "I was one of those little boys who dribbled a ball down a dirt road and dreamed of being a Tiger," said Keith.

He grew up to be a Tiger. At 6-foot-3, he was a fiercely competitive basketball player. He went on to play at junior college, where he was valedictorian, and then moved on to Union College in Barbourville, Kentucky, where he again was valedictorian.

Keith's six brothers and sisters all left the mountains to find adequate work. "So many of our good people have had to leave," he said. "These are the best people in the world. They want to stay, but there are no jobs for them and no chance for them to succeed."

Keith did what he always dreamed of doing. He went back to Manchester to coach basketball. In 1970, after eight years as an assistant coach, he was given a chance to prove his theory that "when these people are given an opportunity, they usually excel."

They have proved him right, winning more than 500 games for him, going to the "Sweet 16" 11 times, and giving Clay County the best winning percentage in Kentucky—85 percent—during his 18 seasons as coach.

Behind Keith's occasional backwoods expressions—he said he was glad to win the state title because "these things are harder to come by than chicken teeth"—is a shrewd coaching mind. He knows his opponent like a book and can work referees like a pump. His commitment to his players is unflagging; he has gotten scholarships, usually to small Kentucky schools, for all but three of the seniors who have played for him the last 17 years.

Keith underwent quadruple bypass surgery in August and has since lost 50 pounds, but his sideline intensity has not diminished. He teaches four consumer math classes a day—students call him "Bobby"—and owns Manchester's most popular men's clothing store. He admits to similarities between his Tigers and the small-town high school that won the 1954

Indiana state basketball championship and was immortalized in the 1986 movie *Hoosiers*.

"We were both from rural areas, we were both small physically, and we both beat big teams from a metro area," he said.

After winning state titles in 1954, '55, and '56, teams from Kentucky's three mountain regions went 29 years before making it to the state finals again in 1985, when Clay County lost to Hopkinsville 65–64. During the quarter-century before Clay County won the '87 state title, mountain teams were eliminated in the first round of the tournament 70 percent of the time.

The mountains' state title drought started in 1957, the year high school athletic competition was integrated in Kentucky. Predominantly black teams from Louisville dominated the "Sweet 16" during the 1960s and 1970s, with Louisville teams winning eight state titles during one 10-year period.

Fittingly, Clay County had to beat a Louisville team to win the "Sweet 16" last year at Rupp Arena in Lexington. The Tigers defeated Ballard High School 76–73 in overtime despite being soundly out-rebounded. Ballard's starters included two 6-foot-6 players, one 6-foot-5, and another 6-foot-3. "I'd rather play the big ones than the little ones," said Chadwell, he of the extraordinary leaping ability. "It just seems like you accomplish more."

The Tigers had won by 20 in the "Sweet 16" semifinals against a Madison Central team with a lineup of players 6-8, 6-5, 6-4, and 6-5. In the quarterfinals, Clay County played before 24,041 people, the largest crowd ever to watch a high school game in the United States.

The Tigers were 35–3 last year and finished the regular season this year at 27–1. Their lone loss was in a December holiday tournament to Eau Claire High School of Columbia, South Carolina, the top-ranked team in South Carolina. Eau Claire started two 6-foot-9 players and another who was 6-foot-7, but the team still only beat Clay County 79–77.

In one incredible, 24-hour period in January—during the Louisville Invitational Tournament—the Tigers defeated the Number 2, 3, and 5 teams in Kentucky. "There's a great deal of pride in the mountains and there's not many things we can say we rank at the top of Kentucky in," said Keith. "But we do in basketball."

Reprinted from Sam Heys, "Hills of Coal, Feats of Clay," *Atlanta Journal-Constitution*, 1988. © With permission of the *Atlanta Journal and Constitution*, P.O. Box 4689, Atlanta, GA 30302.

KENTUCKY

SCHOLARS, A CLASSIC

Basketball is a great leveler. Requiring only five players on a side, it gives the small school a chance at least once in a while. Requiring minimum expenditures in equipment and apparel, it can be played under the meanest of circumstances. When Henry Clay High School of Lexington met Carlisle County High of Bardwell in the 1983 Kentucky state boys' final, there were three and a half times as many people in the crowd than in all Carlisle County. The confrontation, the game, and the atmosphere couldn't have been better dreamed in Hollywood.

It was Ashland vs. Carr Creek all over again. Fifty-five years and three wars had gone by, the game had changed completely, the arena was five times as large, dress and hairdos were different, the press corps had grown beyond wildest predictions, and this time there was television.

But the scenario was the same: the Kentucky state final, big school vs. little school, city vs. country, diehard fans, a white-knuckle multiple-overtime game, a low-scoring defensive battle, and in the end a two-point triumph for Goliath and everlasting glory for David.

In addition, the modern classic was east vs. west, local vs. faraway, fast break vs. deliberate, and vindication for the regular-season raters: it pitted Number 1 against Number 3. The year was 1983. The place was Rupp Arena. The opponents were the favorite, Henry Clay of Lexington (31–2), and Carlisle County (40–3) of Bardwell. Henry Clay High School, in a city of 185,000, had 1,582 students in its three upper grades. Carlisle County High, whose community has a population of less than 1,200, had a four-grade enrollment of 276. The entire county, situated in what Kentuckians call the Jackson Purchase region because it was purchased from the Chickasaw Indians during Andrew Jackson's administration, had a population of only 5,400.

Partisans of every small school in the state empathized with the Carlisle Comets and cheered wildly for them, even if they couldn't have located Bardwell on a map. The Comets were a crowd favorite every time they stepped onto the Rupp Arena floor. But Henry Clay had an emotional tug, too. The wife of its veteran coach, Al Prewitt, who had never won The Big One, had cancer, and the team wanted to win for her. It was the sixth state tournament appearance for Prewitt, who had come closest in 1975 when Henry Clay lost the final to Louisville Male, 74–59.

For the Comets it was a community thing. In a rare departure from the norm, they joined their fans in the stands 40 minutes before the game. They were 300 miles from home, they'd never seen so many people, and, in the words of one of them, "We needed each other." For this classic confrontation, fans were in their seats an hour in advance, sensing drama by the droves and not wishing to miss a moment of it.

Well disciplined and knowing it had the crowd, the Comets made Clay play their game. They had their chances. They led, 29–27, with 1:08 to go in regulation time and had the last shot. They got the tip in each of the first two overtimes and held the ball while Henry Clay stayed in a zone. They missed a 30-footer near the end of Overtime Number 1 and took a 31–29 lead when Keith York slipped underneath for a lay-up with 1:14 remaining in Overtime Number 2. But Greg Bates tied the score with two free throws 28 seconds later. The 6-3 Bates missed two shots in the ensuing seconds, but the Comets couldn't capitalize.

In Overtime Number 3 Carlisle County again got the tip, but this time Henry Clay went into a man-to-man and the tempo quickened. The Comets went ahead, 33–31, with 2:02 remaining, but Jeff Blandon knotted things with two free throws at 1:52. As the clock showed 1:25, the Comets were called for a 5-second violation. Henry Clay then stalled until 9 seconds remained. Blandon called time-out. Steve Miller, Henry Clay's 6-6 center, tried a 17-foot turnaround jumper from the baseline. It missed, but the ball bounced off the rim toward Bates on the side. He scored on a two-hand tip-in at the horn. Henry Clay had won its first state crown.

In the Carlisle County stands, there was first stunned silence, then tears. A little later a ground swell of pride would consume the partisans. Fighting the flu, Carlisle County coach Craynor Slone said that "the only way we could have won was the way we played it." David Henley, who hit four of seven shots from the floor said, "Maybe it just wasn't meant to be." To Henley the saddest note was that the team would never play together again.

Back home, there was a motorcade and more than 400 fans gathered at the high school, which is part of a complex also including middle and elementary schools a mile down Route 1377 from Bardwell. School had been dismissed for the state tournament, with the missed days to be made up at the end of the year. Governor Martha Layne Collins landed by helicopter and spoke at an assembly. Station WPSD-TV of Paducah, 28 miles away, did a 30-minute special on the Comet heroics a Sunday hence.

Carlisle County is on the Mississippi River, and the larger Jackson Purchase area is bounded on three sides by water—the Ohio River to the north and west and Kentucky Lake to the east. With few employment opportunities in Bardwell proper, most of the area residents work at West-vaco Paper Products down U.S. 51 or at tire companies in Mayfield or Union City, Tennessee, 30 and 40 miles away.

The pride engendered by an outstanding athletic team in a small town, particularly one treading water economically, is immeasurable. Representative Carroll Hubbard, in whose district Carlisle County is located, saluted the Comets on the House floor with remarks published in the *Congressional Record*. Following are those remarks:

Mr. Speaker, we have just voted favorably upon H.R. 1149, the Oregon Wilderness Bill, a very important bill to many people in Oregon. We have spent over five hours debating and voting on this legislation.

Permit me less than five minutes to speak on a matter of more interest in my district in Kentucky than the Oregon Wilderness Bill.

Last Saturday night in Lexington, Kentucky, with 19,500 Kentuckians watching in the huge Rupp Arena, a high school basketball team from Carlisle County played one of the big Lexington high schools for the 1983 state championship.

It was David vs. Goliath. Carlisle County, population 5,400, has a high school, grades 9 through 12, with a total enrollment of 276. Lexington Henry Clay, grades 10–12, has an enrollment of 1,582.

After winning 40 out of 43 games and tying the Kentucky high school record for most games won in a season, the Carlisle County Comets, the crowd favorite at every game they played in the state tournament last week, lost the final game to the big Lexington school, 35–33, in three overtimes.

There are only 105 boys in the top three grades at Carlisle County High School. Seven of them — Keith York, Phillip Hall, David Henley, David Rambo, John Tyler, Greg Wilson and Mike Tyler — played in the championship game.

The story of this small school, these players' determination and their going all the way to the state finals was front page news in every Kentucky newspaper yesterday.

So, despite the fact that we're taking another minute here, permit me to congratulate the aforenamed players, school principal Burley Mathis, the excellent and successful head coach Craynor Slone, assistant coaches Frankie Brazzell and Todd Johnson, manager Tommy Clayton, and yes, why not, the cheerleaders, Lana Burgess, Denise Ellegood, Lori Larkins, Melissa Lindsey, Angie Morrison, Jennifer Felts and Patricia Scott.

I speak for thousands of Kentuckians in extending congratulations to Coach Craynor Slone and the Carlisle County High School Comets.

THANK THE PIONEERS

Tales from basketball's early days embellish easily. Most of them don't need any embellishing. There were courts in town halls, garages, barns, and basements. Some of them were so small that the free throw circles almost touched each other. Some could fit crossways on a regulation floor. On the high school front there were promotional and administrative problems unimaginable today. Players, coaches, school officials, fans, and media people owe plenty to the pioneer organizers. This story captures a little of Kentucky's early prep basketball history.

Come back to those gritty pioneer days of yesteryear. Come back to the 1916–26 era in Kentucky when that new, intriguing, totally American game called "basket-ball" was taking hold.

It takes a while before an event attains stature. In 1918 several outstanding eastern and western teams declined invitations to the first Kentucky High School Athletic Association-sponsored state tournament—at Centre College in Danville. They wanted to keep their records unblemished. They were champions of their sections, and what further notoriety did they need? Admission was 50 cents for the entire tournament that year, except that those who provided lodging for members of visiting teams received complimentary tickets.

Lexington won the 1918 championship, prevailing in the final by the baseball score of 16–15. Its victim was Somerset, whose ranks included John Sherman Cooper, later a U.S. senator and ambassador, and James "Red" Roberts, who would become a star on Centre's "Praying Colonels" football team that upset mighty Harvard.

After three years in Danville (two were pre-KHSAA), the state tournament "graduated" to the University of Kentucky's Buell Armory, a 65×35 crackerbox seating 1,000. In 1920 the armory hosted 15 games in 28 hours. Louisville was not represented in the Final 16 because of a board of education rule limiting its schools to two out-of-town trips a season. Lexington won the championship, its third straight, but Danville also claimed the title, basing its position on prestate victories over Lexington and Somerset.

Danville sought not to jeopardize its record in a postseason event not yet accorded all-out respect.

In 1922 there were more incidents. Defending champion Louisville Manual was declared ineligible because it didn't compete in a district tournament. Since Manual and Male were the only Louisville schools belonging to the KHSAA, officials chose to split them and order Manual to play in the Green River district at Owensboro. Manual refused, preferring to meet Male for the Louisville title. The "Sweet 16" still didn't have overriding clout although the National Interscholastic triumph of its champion, Lexington, helped swing the populace.

By 1924 the state tourney moved to UK's Alumni Gym. The good news was that it seated 3,000. The bad news was that smoke from a potbellied stove at the south end of the floor blew at the combatants. Lexington won its fifth championship in 7 years, defeating Fort Thomas, 15–10. At this point in Kentucky, there was no time clock, no 10-second rule, and little newspaper coverage. Quarters were ended with the firing of a pistol. There would be a center jump after each field goal for another 13 years.

In its first of five final-game appearances, Louisville St. Xavier won convincingly in 1926, injecting an element of altruism in the process. With his team leading Danville, 21–7, in the finale, Brother Constant, the St. Xavier coach, sent in his reserves "to give the other team a chance." The final score was St. Xavier 26, Danville 13.

A new era dawned in 1927. For 30 years from that point, the state tournament would be sprinkled with hamlet champions. Names such as Heath, Corinth, Midway, Sharpe, Brooksville, Hazel Green, Inez, Brewers, Cuba, and Carr Creek, which under normal conditions might never be known beyond their county boundaries, became household words across Kentucky. Partway through the new era a strange new ingredient called the "fast break" would surface. At its end there would be consolidation, integration, and a big-school resurgence. But those are other stories.

THE ULTIMATE CINDERELLA

The Carr Creek saga has touched the heartstrings of three generations. Perhaps more than any other story it tells how integral a part high school basketball has become in local and regional cultures. It has the extra advantage of a charming rustic name. Would the Watergate story convey the same intrigue if the break-in had occurred in a building named Insurance Exchange? The following wakes up some echoes of the Carr Creek legend.

Someone said that good Kentucky legends are like good bourbon: they're made out of corn from the hills. The Carr Creek basketball legend is ever vulnerable to embellishment, but when the myths and romantic fiction are stripped away, a veritable storehouse of colorful material remains.

When the unbeaten Creekers fought through five overtimes before bowing to likewise unbeaten and eventual national champion Ashland in the 1928 Kentucky final, they won a million hearts. More significantly they ushered in a new era. The doughty, well-publicized play of the unsung mountaineers, both at Lexington and through the quarterfinals of the National Interscholastic in Chicago, stirred new basketball interest throughout the Commonwealth.

Now about those myths. . .

Myth Number 1 said the 8 squad members constituted the entire male student body. In reality there were 18 boys in the school.

Myth Number 2 said all the boys were related. In reality five were, and three weren't. Center Ben Adams and guard Gurney Adams were brothers, and reserve Herman Adams was their cousin. Guard Zelda Hale and Herman Hale were also brothers. Forwards Shelby Stamper and Gillis Madden and reserve Carson Cornett were not related to anyone on the squad.

Myth Number 3 had the team playing all its games outdoors and barefoot, with one basket attached to a tree and the other to the side of the school. The lads did play outdoors in cooperative weather, but they also had a small 50×30 indoor auditorium court with a 12-foot ceiling. And they did wear shoes.

Myth Number 4 said the Creekers were coached by a Yale engineering graduate or had no coach at all. In reality they were coached by Oscar Morgan, a grade school teacher who had graduated from Centre College in Danville, Kentucky.

Soon sensing the backwoods images they represented in the eyes of adoring city spectators, the colorful Creekers played the role well. They sang mountain ballads for bigwigs in Chicago and thus earned headlines and food galore. Interviewed at the state tournament about the barefoot myth, the team captain confided that "we don't feel handicapped with shoes on."

Captivated by the Creekers' district tournament play but distressed that the lads had to wear T-shirts and cut-down overalls, Richmond fans collected $55 to rectify the situation. When Carr Creek took the floor in Lexington, its standard bearers were clad in spanking new blue-and-white uniforms.

Kentucky's state tournament format in 1928 called for "A" and "B" flights, with the winners meeting in the finale. While all other states except Indiana have since gravitated to at least two classifications, Kentucky has gone the other way, reverting to a single class. But in '28 Carr Creekers were "B," and they rolled. They ripped Walton, 31–11; Minerva, 21–11; and pretourney favorite Lawrenceburg, 37–11, for the class title. Then came the mighty Ashland Tomcats, led by future University of Kentucky standout Ellis Johnson. They'd captured "A" laurels with victories over Danville, 16–8; Henderson, 25–13; and Covington, 22–13.

It was a matchmaker's dream: the greatest team in state history vs. the most colorful, large school vs. small, city (relatively speaking) vs. mountain, high budget (Ashland had warm-up suits) vs. low, the Ashland zone vs. Carr Creek's man-to-man. Four thousand fans filled every seat, aisle, and nook of the UK gym. The underdogs took an early lead and were ahead at halftime by the incredible score of 4–3. The zone vs. man-to-man situation put a clamp on offense. Ashland led 9–6, but a late outside field goal by Madden and a free throw by Stamper knotted things at the end of regulation time. After three scoreless overtimes, Gene Strother scored under the hoop, and Johnson broke out of a full-floor dribbling exhibition to give Ashland a 13–9 lead. Carr Creek controlled the center tip, and a Hale set shot reduced the margin to 13–11. Ashland got the next tip, and Johnson dribbled away the final 60 seconds.

John McGill, noted Kentucky sports historian who has served as sports editor of both the *Lexington Herald* and the *Ashland Daily Independent*, saw the game. He recalls himself as a minority rooter, Johnson as "the perfect player," and the Creekers matching Ashland in poise and determination. Neville Dunn of the *Herald* said "it was the greatest game of basketball ever played in Lexington, bar none."

With the iron hot, fans raised more than enough money to send the Carr Creek lads to the national tournament in Chicago. Enough was left over to cover materials for a new local gymnasium. Coach Morgan said the boys and their parents would build it.

Back home, the Creekers were showered with invitations to banquets, vaudeville shows, and baseball opening games. Representative Fred Vinson praised them in the halls of Congress. Gurney Adams, who became a teacher at his old high school, said, "It was the way everybody was so nice to us that stands out in my memory. Even the team we beat would cheer for us in the next game."

Carr Creek won the state tournament in 1956, the year Kelly Coleman of nearby Wayland upstaged everybody. One might think this team would supplant its '28 counterpart in partisan hearts, but that's not the way life is. The pioneers usually leave the most lasting impact, and that is the way it has been with Carr Creek. Today local youngsters attend Knott County Central High School in Hindman, the county seat and a community also possessed of a distinguished basketball tradition. The county school's enrollment is more than 900, a far cry from the handful who attended old Carr Creek in '28.

TO EXCEL IN SECRET

Clem Haskins coached at his alma mater, Western Kentucky University, before he was hired away by Minnesota. The Louisville team is currently all black. Kentucky, Murray State, and other Commonwealth colleges have featured outstanding blacks in recent years while inner-city high schools from Louisville and Lexington as well as integrated teams from around the state are consistent state tournament contenders. But it wasn't always that way. In fact, anyone over 45 can remember when it wasn't. Here are some highlights of that story.

Prior to 1957 the black basketball experience in Kentucky was akin to that of long-ago Negro League baseball. The teams labored in relative obscurity, and only a small percentage of the citizenry knew the quality that abounded.

In Illinois integration had been gradual. All-black schools in certain areas had been excluded from mainstream tournament participation before 1946, but there had long been integrated teams. In Kentucky the transition was relatively quick.

It was poetic justice that the state's first black team to win The Big One was Louisville Central (1969). Under Coach Willy Kean, Central had compiled an incredible 857–83 record during the 34-year period 1923–56. That's a percentage of .911! Central had won seven state Negro championships and been runner-up in 10 other years. The 1969 achievement was a long-held dream come true.

It took patient philosophers to coach black high school teams before and just after integration. To retaliate stridently at name-calling would ruin the future, reasoned S.T. Roach, coach of the outstanding Lexington Dunbar teams that posted a 512–142 record from 1940 through 1965. Trips presented special problems. There weren't many restaurants between cities where blacks could be served; that meant brown bagging it. There weren't many places where they could stay once they had reached their destination. But coaches and players learned to live with the system. Most of them say the experiences brought teams and student bodies closer together. Some of the most hospitable game stops were in the southeastern section of the

141

state, notably Breathitt County, Hindman, and Carr Creek. The coaches remember these things.

Black coaches had special responsibilities in the old society. Roach, for example, was a strict disciplinarian who demanded gentlemanly behavior. His creed was: "If you can't be a gentleman *and* play, you can't play."

For 25 years prior to 1957, the black Kentucky High School Athletic League (KHSAL) paralleled the mainstream Kentucky High School Athletic Association (KHSAA). Similarly it divided the state into districts and regionals, and its state tournament also became a 16-team affair. While rivals Louisville Central and Lexington Dunbar dominated the KHSAL tourneys, there were many other powerhouses. Lincoln Institute of Shelby County won three times while Horse Cave Colored, Hopkinsville Attucks, Madisonville Rosenwald, and Mayo-Underwood of Frankfort won twice each.

As with any drastic change, however right, integration had a downside. It caused the demise of the KHSAL, the loss of jobs, and the loss of a camaraderie that only the involved coaches could ever understand. From an athletic standpoint there was a mighty upside. Black stars could now be showcased as never before. Of all the black high schools, Lexington Dunbar made the biggest initial impact on the KHSAA tournament, qualifying for the "Sweet 16" six times from 1958 to 1965 and placing second in '61 and '63.

How many Wes Unselds, Darrell Griffiths, Dirk Minniefields, and Clem Haskinses were there in the days before integration when neither the northern colleges nor the NBA sought black players? We'll never know. Baseball fans have mild knowledge of Satchel Paige, Josh Gibson, and Buck Leonard, but the feats of early black basketball stars in the South are, for the most part, lost in antiquity.

OUT OF STRIFE

As with war and politics, the inside story of an athletic season often remains unknown to fans until a generation has gone by. The record book shows that Lexington Lafayette, coached by the storied Ralph Carlisle, won the 1953 Kentucky boys' championship, but it doesn't mention the seemingly endless problems the team experienced during the season. Robert T. Garrett's story in the Louisville Courier-Journal, *written as 10 of the '53 champions held their 30th reunion on occasion of another state tournament, captures the nostalgia.*

They were Lexington's golden boys in what was, for middle-class America at least, a golden era.

The 12 boys from suburban Lafayette High School overcame local skepticism, internal strife and injuries to steamroll four opponents and win the 1953 state basketball championship.

They pocketed keys to the city, paraded through the streets, preened through weeks of victory celebrations and papered their bedroom walls with certificates declaring them Kentucky Colonels and honorary Lions Club members.

During the 30 years since that high-water mark in their lives, most of them haven't exactly set the world on fire.

But, defying the stereotypes cast by playwright Jason Miller in his smash success, *That Championship Season*, they haven't been a collection of shipwrecks either.

Most of the members of the 1953 Lafayette Generals' championship team gathered for a 30-year reunion at Rupp Arena yesterday to relive their triumph.

And all appeared to be solid citizens and upright family men. In fact, they seem like parsons next to former head coach Ralph Carlisle.

Carlisle, 68, who steered Lafayette to three state titles and who was voted the Number 1 coach in the Sweet 16 Hall of Fame, remains as mischievous as ever.

And his 1953 team, which the late Adolph Rupp proclaimed at the time as "the best high school team I've seen in Kentucky in the 23 years I've been here," remains loyal to its mentor.

At least, that is, the 12 members of the team who survived the stormy 1952–53 season to its happy conclusion.

Ranked Number 1 in the state in preseason polls, the 1953 Generals lost six of their first dozen or so regular season games. A desperate Carlisle tried 17 different combinations of starting players before the team hit its stride in post-season play.

But that winning stride was attained only after Carlisle had removed three of his top eight players from the team for curfew violations and insubordination. Amid threats of lawsuits and heavy pressure from what was in those pre-consolidation days the Fayette County school board, Carlisle put the decision to his remaining players.

"We voted unanimously to support the coach's decision and not to have them come back," recalled Steve Shuck, a senior guard on the squad at the time.

"It was a very difficult time, but we pulled together after that, and there was no more turmoil," added Shuck, who is now assistant athletic director of the Princeton (Ohio) school system.

More trouble lay ahead, however. The team's best set-shooter, Norris "Chigger" Flynn, now a Lexington insurance adjuster, broke his arm for the second year in a row as tourney-time approached.

"I kept stats after that," said Flynn, whose 5-foot-5 stature made him an anomaly on a team regarded in its day as one of the tallest ever in Kentucky.

After winding up regular play with a 16–6 record, the Generals twice trounced their city rivals, the Henry Clay Blue Devils, to win a "Sweet 16" berth. (Henry Clay's star guard that year, Al Prewitt, is now its head coach and led the Blue Devils to the finals of the Boys' State High School Basketball Tournament last night in Lexington.)

In those days, when Lexington was a city of fewer than 60,000 that still had racially segregated schools, the Generals and Blue Devils tended to ignore all-black Dunbar High School and to take only one another seriously.

Lafayette went on to handily crush Allen County, undefeated Clay County, Newport Catholic, and giant-killer Paducah Tilghman to win the crown.

The "Big Brass," as the team was known, was led by 6-foot-9 center Bill "Willow William" Florence (now an employee at IBM Corporation's Lexington plant) and 6-foot-3 guard Vernon Hatton (now an auctioneer and real-estate agent in Lexington).

Hatton, who went on to be an All-America at the University of Kentucky and to spend four years in the pros, recalled yesterday that Carlisle sent in his reserve players early in the second half of each of the General's 1953 "Sweet 16" appearances.

"In the final against Paducah Tilghman, we were up by about 20 points at half," Hatton said.

"Coach came into the locker room to give us a pep talk, and said, 'Fellas, (Paducah Tilghman coach) Otis Dinning is a good friend of mine, so everybody is going to play plenty this half.' "

Largely as a result, Lafayette's star players set few tournament records. But the team held the record for many years for most points scored in the tournament and in the championship game.

Described in press reports at the time as Lafayette's "baby-faced killers" and a "murderous execution squad," the 1953 Generals were a physically punishing and highly disciplined squad.

Carlisle played under Rupp at UK and retains some bitterness that he never got to coach in the college ranks. Yesterday he scoffed at some of the play during semifinal action at Rupp Arena.

"It's what I used to call 'YMCA ball,' " he said. Only a few modern-day teams, such as that of Carlisle County High that made the finals last night, play with enough defense, control, and discipline to suit him, Carlisle said.

Of his 1953 starting five, two players have continued to pursue sports careers. Doug Shively, who was a 6-foot-3 forward, concentrated on football, not basketball, and is now coach of the Arizona Wranglers in the new U.S. Football League. Don Plunkett, another 6-foot-3 forward, is now a race starter at thoroughbred tracks around the country.

Walter Newtown, who was a 5-foot-11 starting guard, is an engineer in Lexington as is reserve forward Ed Stipp.

The fabled Generals bench of 1953 also included Ron Hacker, now a golf pro in Woodford County; Don Hopper, a Lexington pharmacist who is also a commodity broker; Ed Selliers, an algebra teacher and baseball coach at Bryan Station High School in Lexington; John Peck, an engineer at IBM in Lexington; and Gerald "Babe" Walton, a Lexington home builder.

Ten of the former players gathered for dinner last night. Hacker and Shively didn't attend. The 10 then went to watch another champion be crowned at Rupp Arena, from seats high in the upper deck that caused some to grumble about how quickly a town's heroes are forgotten. Henry Clay defeated Carlisle [County] 35-33 in triple overtime.

Carlisle said he had known all along that his 1953 team was championship material.

Of his glory years in the early 1950s at Lafayette, Carlisle said he had only two regrets.

One was his handling of John Y. Brown, Jr., class of '52, a future millionaire and governor who rode Carlisle's bench throughout his playing career.

"If I had known then what I know now, he (Brown) would have played a lot more," Carlisle said.

The other misgiving was his handling of the 1953 suspension of three of his players.

"If I had to do it over again, I would be a bigger person about it all and I would have prevented those boys from being what they were by handling them in a different way.

"You see, I only saw black and white in those days. And now I see gray."

Reprinted from Robert T. Garrett, "A Sweet Era: Lexington's 'Golden Boys' Meet to Court the Old Days," *Louisville Courier-Journal*, March 20, 1983. © With permission of Courier-Journal and Louisville Times Co., 1989.

KENTUCKY
POTPOURRI

*Superlatives, oddities, and memorable anecdotes
collected over the years from Kentucky*

When you outscore your opponents, 39–17, from the floor, you can usually expect a decisive victory. The boys of Louisville Shawnee did that on January 15, 1972, against Powell County in Stanton, yet lost the game by 7 points, 104–97! This was a night for the record books. Powell County converted 70 of 89 free throws, both breaking national high school records. By contrast, visiting Shawnee made 19 of 36.

The postgame remarks of Shawnee coach James Gordon were a masterpiece of subdued reaction. Instead of harping on the gross imbalance in foul-calling or making even a remote reference to hometown officiating, he simply said the game "will help us get ready for the Louisville Invitational; we know we will have to play some teams from out in the state."

Picking athletes for stardom at the next level of play has always been difficult and was particularly so in the transitional forties. The process is complicated by team considerations. If it's a so-called one-man team, will the phenom fit into a role at the college level? If it's an honest-to-goodness five-man team, who's better than whom, and do any of them possess the skills to make it later on?

One of the standouts in Kentucky's 1940 state tournament was Joe Fulks of little Kuttawa, a Lake Barkley community of about 450 people. He scored 13 points in a first-round 28–26 loss to Morganfield. Six years later—after Western Kentucky and the Marine Corps—Fulks became the first superstar of the postwar pros (in the BAA, forerunner of the NBA). Unheralded and featuring a two-hand jump shot, he led all scorers in 1946–47 with a 23.2 average in 60 games for the champion Philadelphia Warriors. He was scoring runner-up in two subsequent campaigns, and his 63 points against the Indianapolis Jets on February 10, 1949, in the Philadelphia Arena stood as the pro league's single-game record for 10 years.

Losing a coin toss was a major factor in Lexington's winning the 1922 National Interscholastic championship at the University of Chicago. The Blue Devils started slowly, escaping with a pair of 1-point victories. Prior to their third assignment—against Cathedral of Duluth, Minnesota—a problem arose: both teams wore blue jerseys. Lexington lost the toss and was given the only available numbered shirts, those of the University of Chicago varsity. As a result, the Blue Devils drew enthusiastic, almost unanimous support from the Chicago crowd. They whipped Cathedral, 37–26, and hit a stride that swept them to the title. After considerable postgame arguing, the Lexington fans persuaded Director Amos Alonzo Stagg to part with the lucky jerseys, and they were carried back to Lexington as additional trophies.

The winningest current basketball coach in the college ranks—and believed to be the second winningest of all time—is a native Kentuckian whose feats remain relatively secret.

His statistics seldom appear in the college lists because his school is in Division II. He isn't remembered as a basketball luminary in his native state because he specialized in football at his Paducah high school from 1937 to 1941. He used the court sport simply as an off-season conditioner. At Morgan State University football was still his game.

The man is Clarence "Bighouse" Gaines of Winston-Salem State University in North Carolina. He posted his 800th victory on January 24, 1990, when Winston-Salem defeated Livingstone, 79–70. If Gaines is remembered for anything outside the Carolinas, it is for his NCAA College Division championship in 1967 and his famous pupil, Earl "The Pearl" Monroe.

Eddie Robinson caught Bear Bryant in football. The speculation is whether "Bighouse," 66 years old when he reached the 800th milestone, will hang around long enough to pick up the 75 additional wins needed to pass Adolph Rupp.

Those who decry overemphasis on sports at the high school level and the pressures placed on adolescent athletes would have found endless ammunition in 1956. As the colorful Kelly Coleman of Wayland, averaging 46.9 points a game, prepared for his first "Sweet 16" game in Lexington, fans entered the arena attached to helium-filled balloons reading "COLEMAN" and a screaming headline in the local *Herald* asked, "Kan King Kelly Kop Kommonwealth Kage Krown?" There was a big resentment factor. A sizable segment of the crowd booed every time Coleman touched the ball. He responded with 185 points in his team's four Lexington games, including 68 in Wayland's third-place triumph. He left the arena in a tiff. His sister accepted his all-tournament trophy.

Decisions change lives. Ray Bowling of Laurel County High in London had had his fill of basketball coaching, all of which had been with boys. He'd been away from the game for a few years and didn't want to go back. But when Superintendent Hayward Gilliam insisted in 1974 that Bowling coach the girls, he relented. The rest is a glowing chapter in Kentucky prep history. Over the next 10 seasons Bowling took the Lady Cardinals of Laurel County to three consecutive state championships (1977, '78, '79), six trips to the state tournament, and a record 73 straight victories. His teams put Kentucky girls' basketball on the map.

Nowhere is school consolidation more evident than in Kentucky. Unlike Illinois, which has 51 public high schools with fewer than 100 students at this writing, Kentucky has virtually none. The word "County"—for example, "Clay County," "Shelby County," and "Laurel County," all recent state tournament winners—is per se part of the names of 92 of the state's high schools. In several other cases, such as "Knox Central" and "South Hopkins," the county name is present and at least a substantial county area is implied.

Picturesque team nicknames in Kentucky include several of historical, mythological, or environmental connotation. Notable are the Fulton County Pilots, Lafayette Generals, Sacred Heart Valkyries, Harrison County Thorobreds, Pineville Mountain Lions, and St. Francis Wyverns. How many St. Francis fans, much less its opponents, know that a "wyvern" is a winged, two-legged creature with a dragon's head?

Other inventive Kentucky nicknames are the Corbin Redhounds, Villa Madonna Vixens, Notre Dame Pandas, Dayton Green Devils, Bracken County Polar Bears, Mercy Missiles, Lloyd Memorial Juggernauts, Somerset Briar Jumpers, Central City Golden Tide, McDowell Dare Devils, and Lone Oak (Paducah) Purple Flash.

The 10 most striking upsets in Kentucky prep basketball history, as selected by veteran observer John McGill, span a 63-year period. McGill confesses that memories fail and that he has probably omitted a few "musts," but here, in chronological order, are his nominations:

1927—Millersburg Military School 34, London 25 (state final)

1930—Corinth 22, Kavanaugh 20 (state final)

1938—Sharpe 26, Louisville St. Xavier 23 (state tournament)

1943—Hindman 29, Louisville St. Xavier 26 (state final)

1944—Olive Hill 23, undefeated Brooksville 20 (state tournament)

1956—Carr Creek 68, Wayland 67 (state tournament); Carr Creek 72, Henderson 68 (state final)

1958—Daviess County 59, Clark County 56 (state tournament)

1961—Lexington Lafayette 59, Ashland 58 (regular season; only loss for 36–1 state champion Ashland, rated state's all-time strongest team by 1987 poll of writers and coaches)

1984—Logan County 70, Lexington Clay 68 (state tournament; Clay was defending champion and ranked Number 1)

Most of the Cinderella schools in Kentucky's long-ago are gone now, either in the flesh or in name. One of the most memorable was Kavanaugh High in Lawrenceburg. It was founded and sustained by the amazing Rhoda Kavanaugh. She walked the sidelines during games carrying an umbrella. In the classroom she taught geometry, algebra, Latin, French, history, and grammar. You knew who was in charge. Kavanaugh High, coached by Faire Jones, came close to glory in 1930. It won the state Class A final, then lost to the B winner, Corinth, on a shot from near midcourt in the final seconds.

Most highly advertised individual duels prove disappointing. One of the phenoms will dominate. One, aided by a superior supporting cast, will exploit a weakness in the other. Or one will have a bad night or not be up to physical par. But when Kelly Coleman of Wayland met Corky Withrow of Georgetown in 1956, no one was disappointed. They hit 40 points apiece as Georgetown handed Wayland one of its rare defeats.

It has been said that high school coaches coach, college coaches recruit, and pro coaches motivate. If this oversimplification is even partially valid, why do so few outstanding high school coaches receive college opportunities? Not every prep coach aspires to the hurly-burly of recruiting and other responsibilities peculiar to the college scene. But some, such as Ralph Carlisle, did. He compiled a 488–144 record over 24 seasons punctuated by three state titles at Lexington Lafayette, but no college ever made a reasonable offer. His coaching salary in 1961 was $5,070, and he was working several jobs. So he quit coaching. He may not have enjoyed selling life insurance, but he made almost $36,000 in his first year at it.

Illinois has its Hebron, with Cobden and Braidwood in the shadows. Indiana has its Milan, along with Wingate, Argos, and Cloverdale. But few states have had as lengthy a string of "Little Davids" such as Kentucky produced during the 29-year period 1928 through 1956. That era began and ended with Carr Creek, the tiny mountain school that was consolidated out of existence in 1974. The Creekers settled for second place in the '28 state tourney but won in '56. State champions during the era emerged from such small towns as Heath (1929), Corinth (1930), Midway (1937), Sharpe (1938), Brooksville (1939), Hazel Green (1940), Inez (1941 and 1954), Hindman (1943), Brewers (1948), and Cuba (1952). Runners-up in the period included Corinth (1929), Tolu (1931), Horse Cave (1933), Nebo (1936), Inez (1937), Hindman (1939), Brewers (1947), and Cuba (1951).

While teams from the eastern mountains are generally perceived as the most colorful, the western and central standard bearers had their moments. Heath, in the far west section, practiced outdoors except once a week when the lads traveled to Paducah or La Center for drills. When no local phone lines were open after the triumph of Sharpe, also in the Paducah area, the good news was borne into town via a call to a neighboring community, then rowboating across a swollen river, then horseback. In 1937 little Midway, out of the Lexington area, introduced something radically different and not immediately popular. It was called the "fast break." It was an early glimpse of things to come.

At the 1941 state tournament Coach Carl Johnson of Hardin found an easy way to protect his players against the city lights of Lexington. He locked their shoes in a closet and went to a movie.

Coach Jock Sutherland, not to be confused with the mentor of the University of Pittsburgh football juggernauts of the thirties, loved his calling but vowed to quit as soon as he won The Big One, the state tournament. He took several teams to the "Sweet 16" during stints at Gallatin County, Harrison County, and Lexington Lafayette over a 23-year period, but something always happened.

By 1979 he had the ingredients, notably a guard combination of Junior Johnson and Dirk Minniefield, later of the University of Kentucky and the NBA. His defense was known as "Jailhouse Junk," with the guards left on their own. How could the opponent know what they were going to do if the coach himself didn't? Before 23,000 spectators in Rupp Arena, the Generals defeated Grant County, Caverna, and Warren East to set up the final against Christian County. Sutherland was one game from the Promised Land.

The Generals led only 31–30 in the first minute of the third quarter but quickly opened a 15-point gap. One hesitates to jump the gun or take things for granted in a fast-moving sport like basketball, but with four minutes remaining and his team holding a 15-point lead, Sutherland's good judgment told him that the magic moment had arrived: the Generals were in. He called time, hugged his wife, and told assistant Don Harville he was turning the coaching reins over to him. The Generals won, 62–52. It was their 36th victory in 37 games and the 465th of Sutherland's career.

The worst flood in local memory almost kept the Breathitt County boys' team out of the 1963 state tournament. Seven of the players, residing in areas 15 miles from the school, were rescued by amphibious "ducks" of the U.S. Corps of Engineers.

As gambling scandals at CCNY, Bradley, LIU, Manhattan, Toledo, and Kentucky in 1950 and 1951 threatened to destroy college basketball, so gamblers cast occasional insidious shadows on the high school game. Big money was bet, and coaches had various methods of combating the scourge. Letcher Norton of Clark County High took the physical route one night during his '51 state championship season. One of his former players had offered three current team members $1,000 each if they would shave the spread to three points. A hanger-on told Norton that the players wanted to talk to him. Norton sent for the fixer, gave him a beating, and sent him packing. At 6-1 and 200-plus the coach was still a tower of strength despite his age, 61. Nine months later the University of Kentucky point-shaving scandal hit the papers.

Adolph Rupp left Freeport (Illinois) High School for the University of Kentucky largely because of a conversation with a gas station owner. He had been unimpressed by the UK environment, and he was riding success in Freeport where the community was savoring a 20–4 record and a third-place state tournament finish. Too, his principal reminded Rupp that Freeport's gym was superior to UK's and that the salary ($2,800) was the same.

But the Freeport station owner looked at it this way: "You can always get a better job from Kentucky; it's rare for a high school coach to get a college call." So Adolph pulled up stakes, and he never had to look for another job. At UK he posted more victories that any college basketball coach in history, 874.

EPILOGUE

High school athletics is athletics in its most idealistic form. As with any worthwhile activity, its officials must constantly battle abuses, but the scales are tipped mightily on the positive side. For every star athlete who is "given a pass" academically during his high school years and is thus shortchanged in the long run, there are a hundred diligent students who benefit immeasurably from the disciplines and experiences of interschool competition.

While Division I colleges wallow in massive recruiting corruption and reap profits undreamable a generation ago, the high schools quietly ply their trade under modest circumstances, teaching the basics to community youngsters, fostering a spirit seldom equaled at higher academic levels, and once in a blue moon producing a superstar.

"Why is there such passion for *high school* basketball?" a visitor to the Illinky region asked. "The pro and college teams are obviously superior." Sir, it's hard to explain, except that the passion is part of American life, particularly in Illinois, Indiana, and Kentucky. It is most evident during "March Madness," a phenomenon that spawned an oft-quoted 1942 poem by H.V. Porter, executive secretary of the National Federation of State High School Associations, who was a noted equipment innovator, former coach, and former executive of the Illinois High School Association. Written with a Robert W. Service lilt during a difficult World War II year when the values of school athletics were subjected to close examination, it reflects the fervor and sportsmanship of state tournaments. It's titled "The Modern Ides of March," and it could just as well have been written by a Hoosier or Kentuckian:

> *The gym lights gleam like a beacon beam*
> *And a million motors hum*
> *In a good will flight on a Friday night,*
> *For basketball beckons, ''Come!''*
> *A sharp-shooting mite is king tonight.*
> *The Madness of March is running.*
> *The winged feet fly, the ball sails high,*
> *And field goal hunters are gunning.*

The colors clash as silk suits flash
And race on a shimmering floor.
Repressions die, and partisans vie
In a goal acclaiming roar.
On Championship Trail toward holy grail
All fans are birds of a feather.
It's fiesta night, and cares lie light
When the air is full of leather.

Since time began, the instincts of man
Prove cave men and current men kin.
On tournament night the sage and wight
Are relatives under the skin.
It's festival time, sans ken or rhyme,
But with nation-wide appeal.
In a cyclone of hate, our ship of state
Rides high on an even keel.

With war nerves tense, the final defense
Is the courage, strength and will
In a million lives where freedom thrives
And liberty lingers still.
Now eagles fly and heroes lie
Beneath some foreign arch.
Let their sons tread when hate is dead
In this happy madness of March!